D0498020

The Misadventures of SALEM HYDE

4

Dinosaur Dilemma

Frank Cammuso

AMULET BOOKS
NEW YORK

PUBLISHER'S NOTE: This is a work of fiction. Names, characters, places, and incidents are either the product of the author's imagination or are used fictitiously, and any resemblance to actual persons, living or dead, business establishments, events, or locales is entirely coincidental.

Hardcover ISBN: 978-1-4197-1534-1
Paperback ISBN: 978-1-4197-1535-8

Book design by Frank Cammuso and Alyssa Nassner

Published in 2015 by Amulet Books, an imprint of ABRAMS.

Printed and bound in China
10 9 8 7 6 5 4 3 2 1

ABRAMS
THE ART OF BOOKS SINCE 1949
115 West 18th Street
New York, NY 10011
www.abramsbooks.com

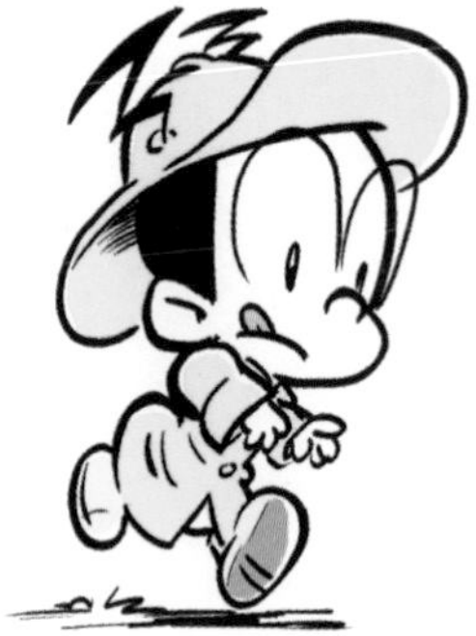

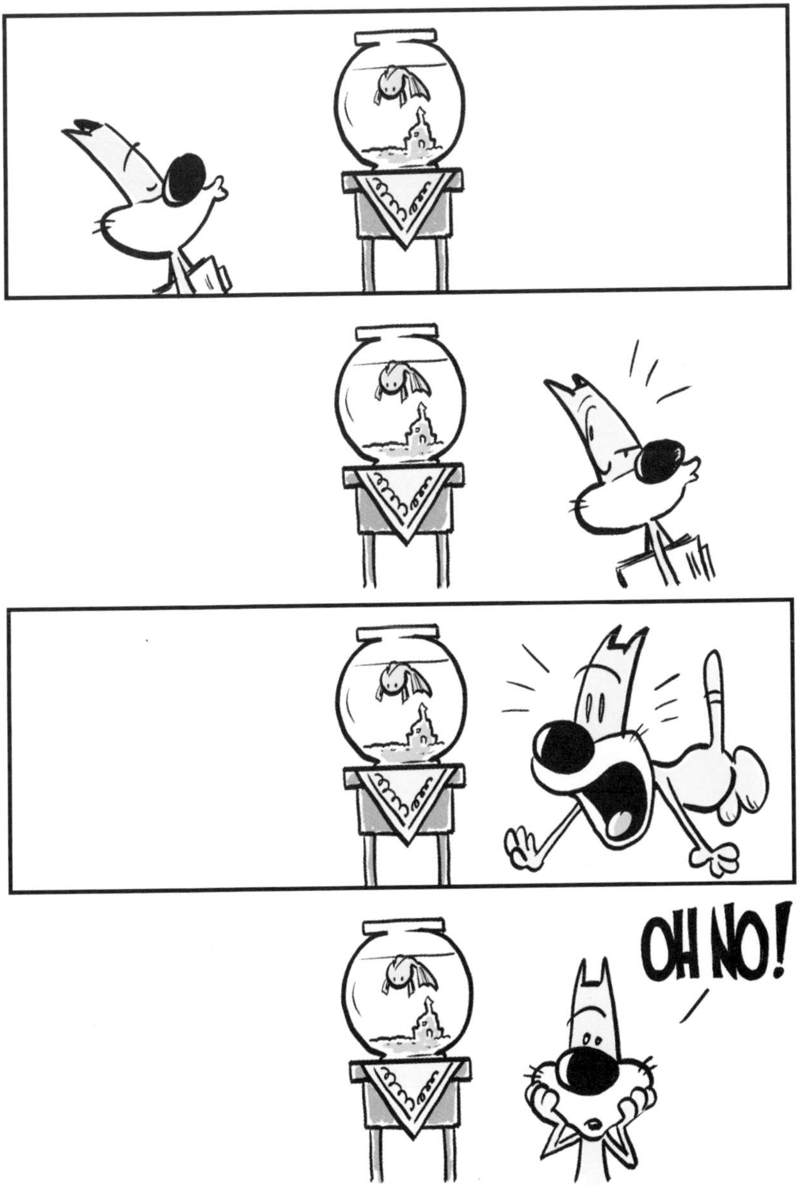
OH NO!

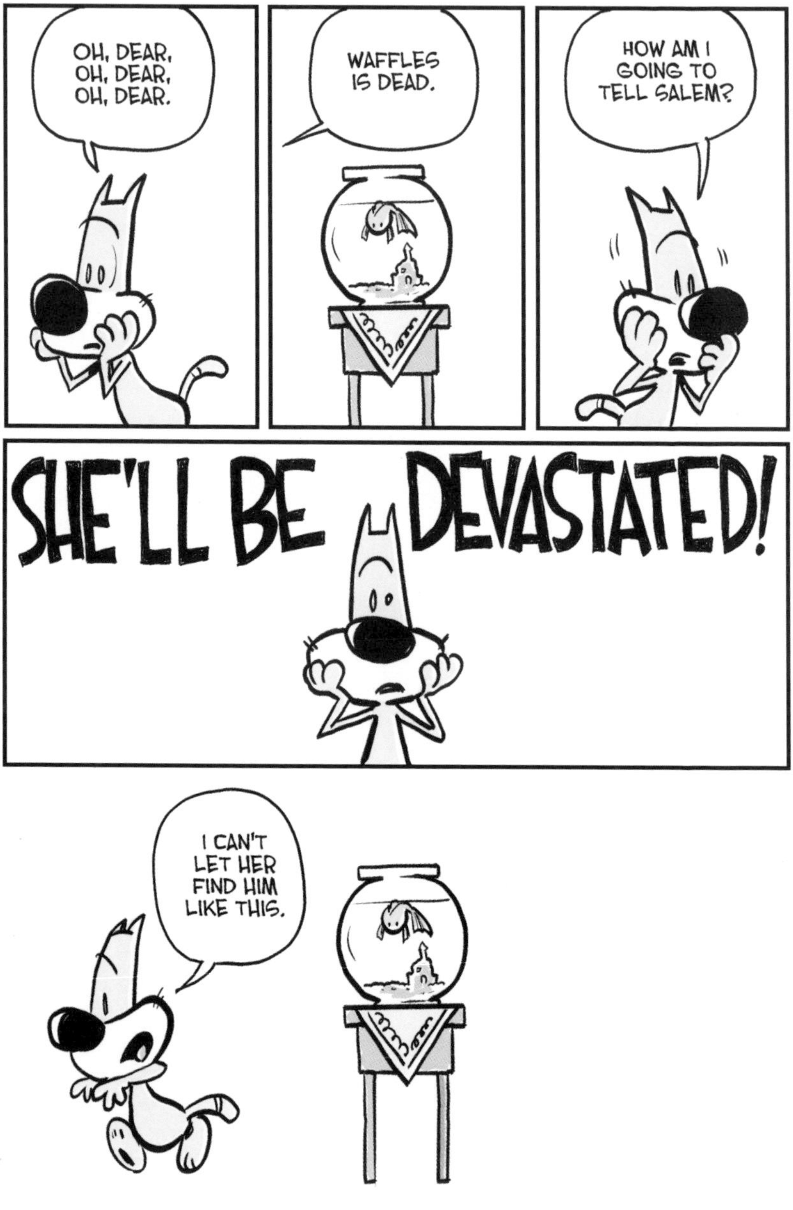
OH, DEAR, OH, DEAR, OH, DEAR.
WAFFLES IS DEAD.
HOW AM I GOING TO TELL SALEM?
SHE'LL BE DEVASTATED!
I CAN'T LET HER FIND HIM LIKE THIS.

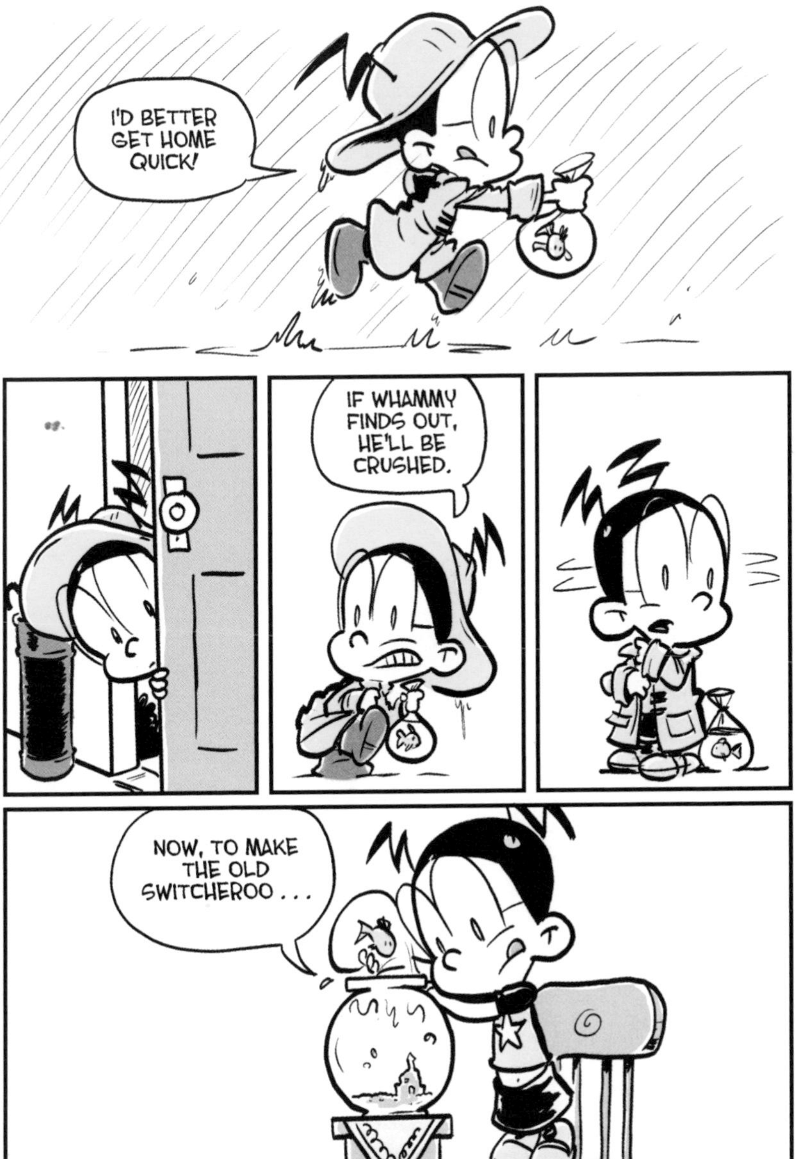
I'D BETTER GET HOME QUICK!
IF WHAMMY FINDS OUT, HE'LL BE CRUSHED.
NOW, TO MAKE THE OLD SWITCHEROO . . .

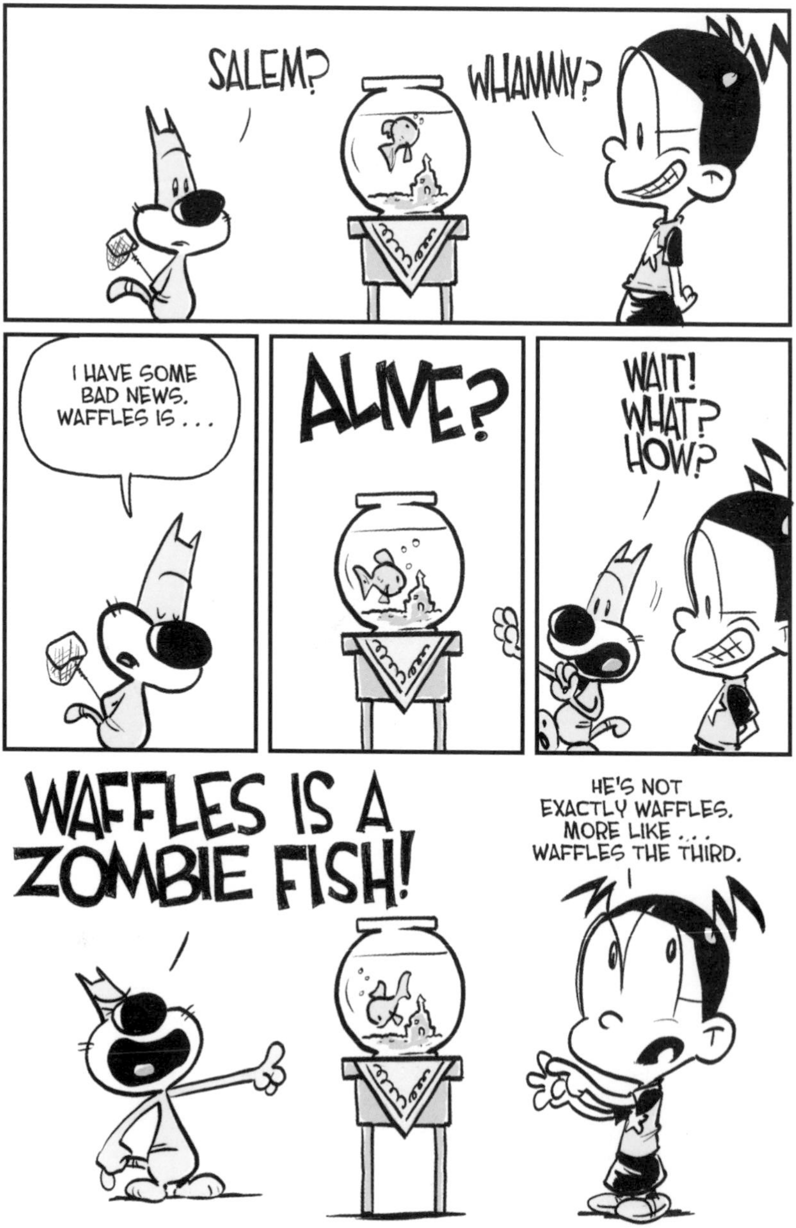

SALEM?
WHAMMY?
I HAVE SOME BAD NEWS. WAFFLES IS . . .
ALIVE?
WAIT! WHAT? HOW?
WAFFLES IS A ZOMBIE FISH!
HE'S NOT EXACTLY WAFFLES. MORE LIKE . . . WAFFLES THE THIRD.

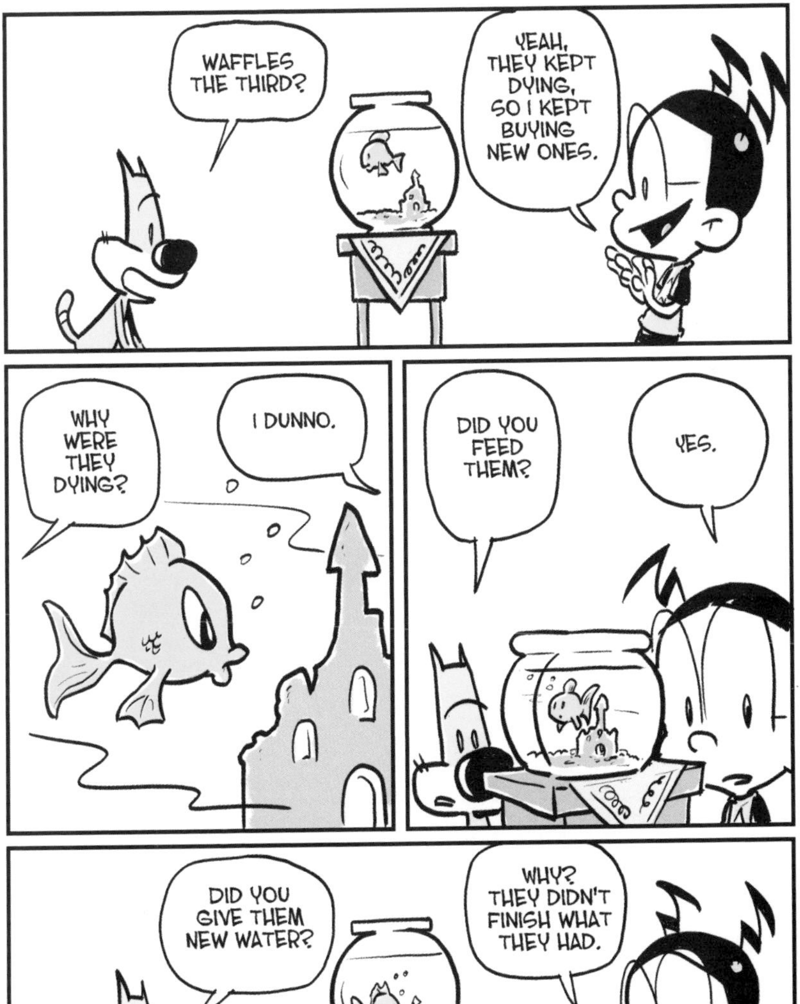
WAFFLES THE THIRD?
YEAH, THEY KEPT DYING, SO I KEPT BUYING NEW ONES.
WHY WERE THEY DYING?
I DUNNO.
DID YOU FEED THEM?
YES.
DID YOU GIVE THEM NEW WATER?
WHY? THEY DIDN'T FINISH WHAT THEY HAD.

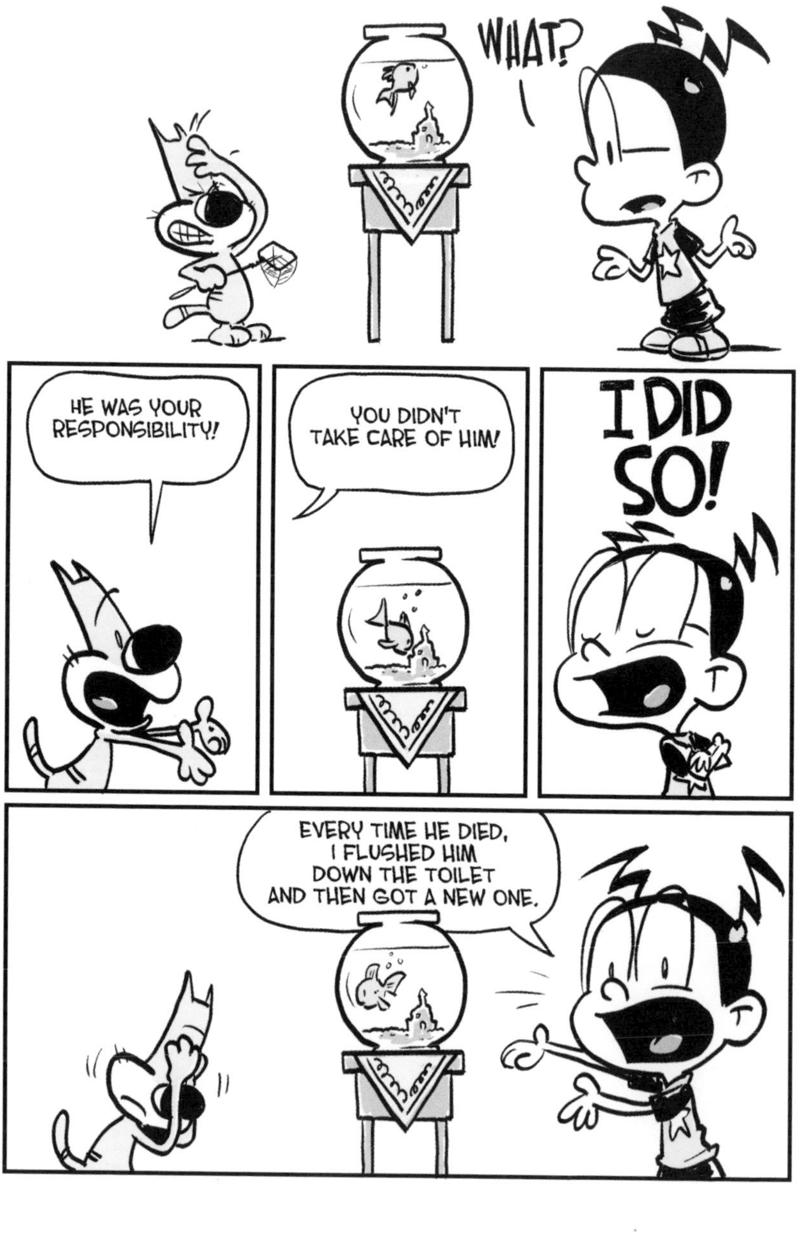
WHAT?
HE WAS YOUR RESPONSIBILITY!
YOU DIDN'T TAKE CARE OF HIM!
I DID SO!
EVERY TIME HE DIED, I FLUSHED HIM DOWN THE TOILET AND THEN GOT A NEW ONE.

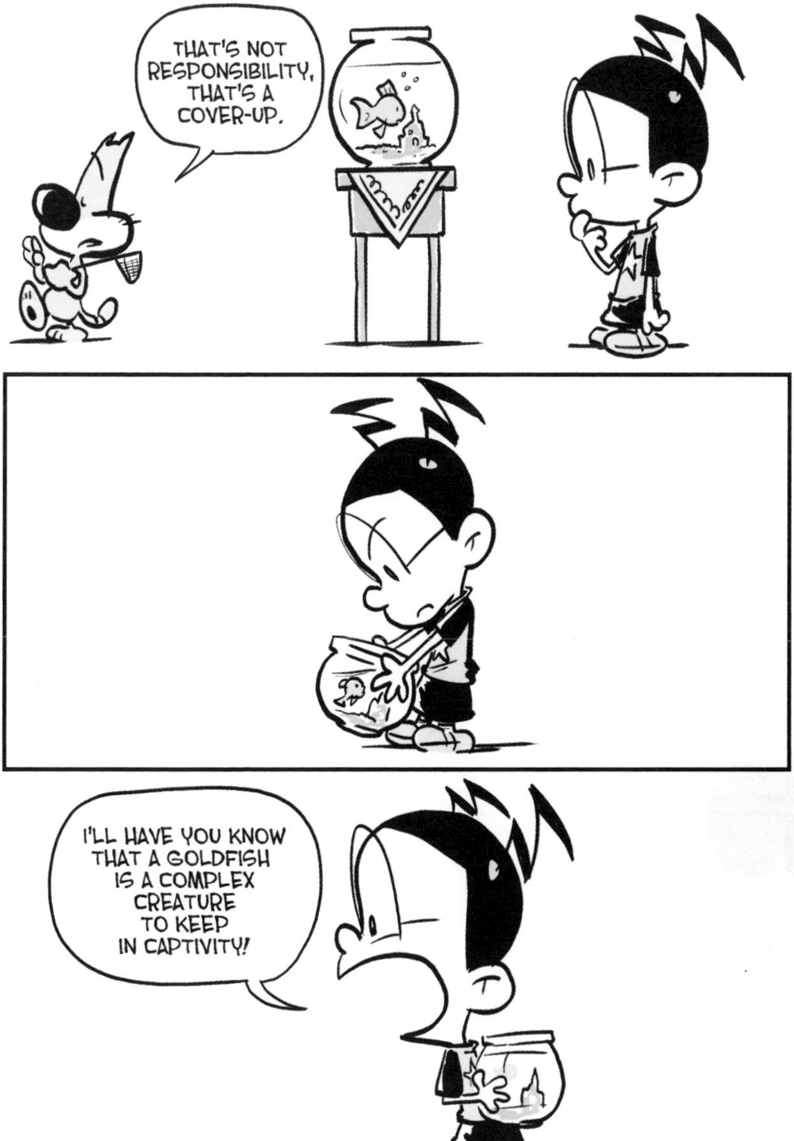
THAT'S NOT RESPONSIBILITY, THAT'S A COVER-UP.
I'LL HAVE YOU KNOW THAT A GOLDFISH IS A COMPLEX CREATURE TO KEEP IN CAPTIVITY!

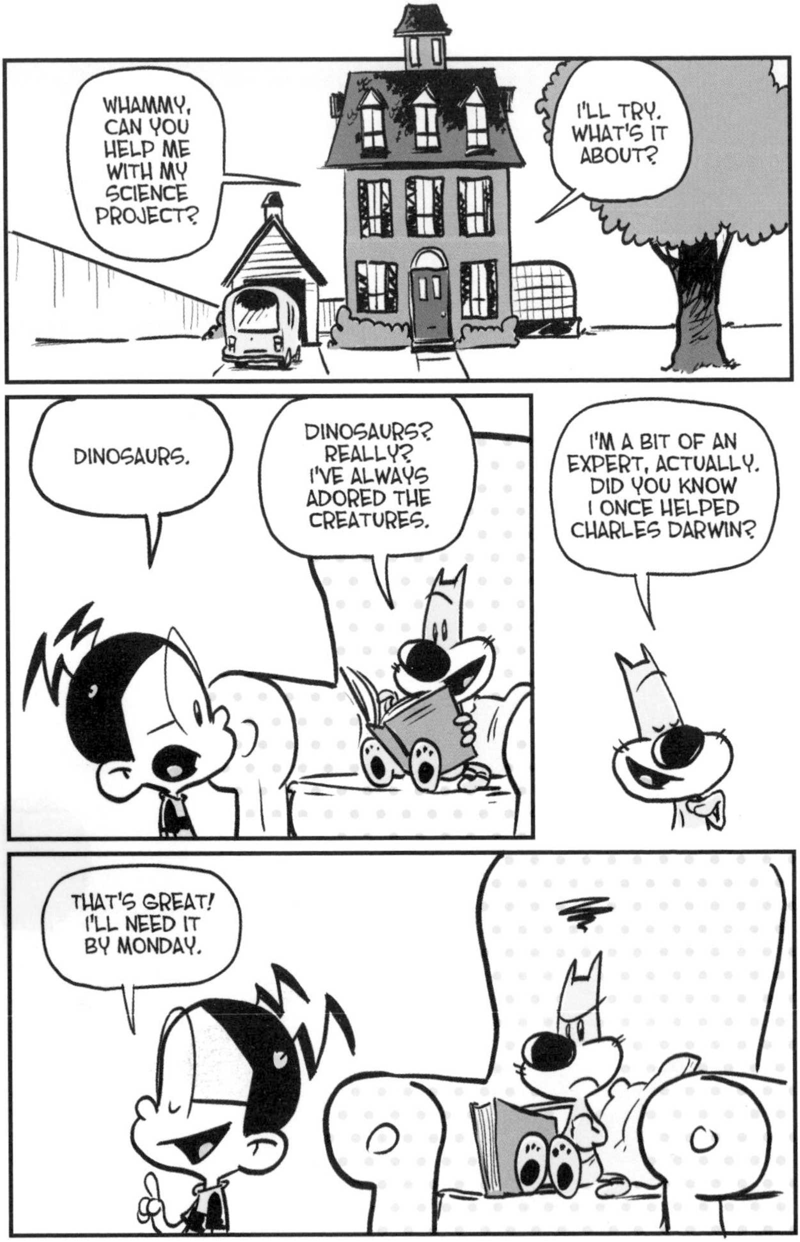
WHAMMY, CAN YOU HELP ME WITH MY SCIENCE PROJECT?
I'LL TRY. WHAT'S IT ABOUT?
DINOSAURS.
DINOSAURS? REALLY? I'VE ALWAYS ADORED THE CREATURES.
I'M A BIT OF AN EXPERT, ACTUALLY. DID YOU KNOW I ONCE HELPED CHARLES DARWIN?
THAT'S GREAT! I'LL NEED IT BY MONDAY.

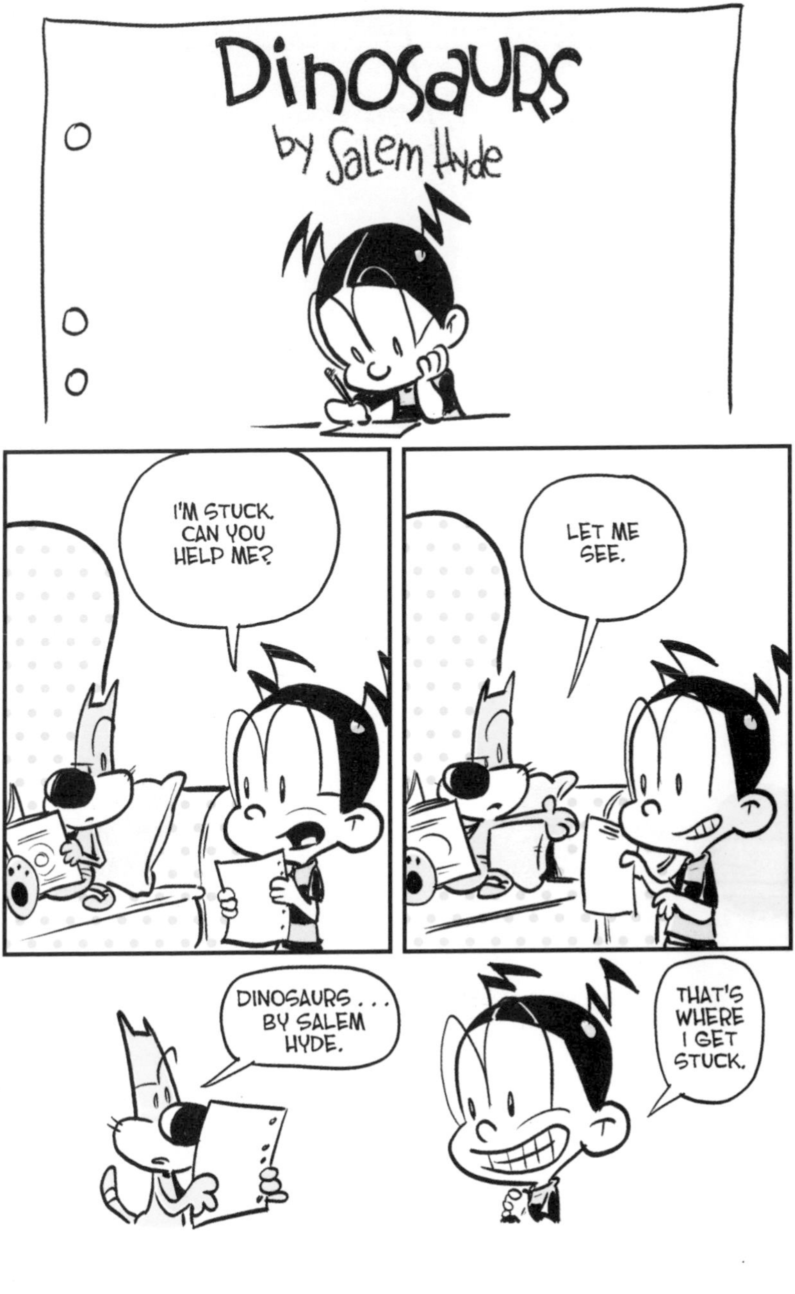
Dinosaurs
by Salem Hyde
I'M STUCK. CAN YOU HELP ME?
LET ME SEE.
DINOSAURS . . . BY SALEM HYDE.
THAT'S WHERE I GET STUCK.

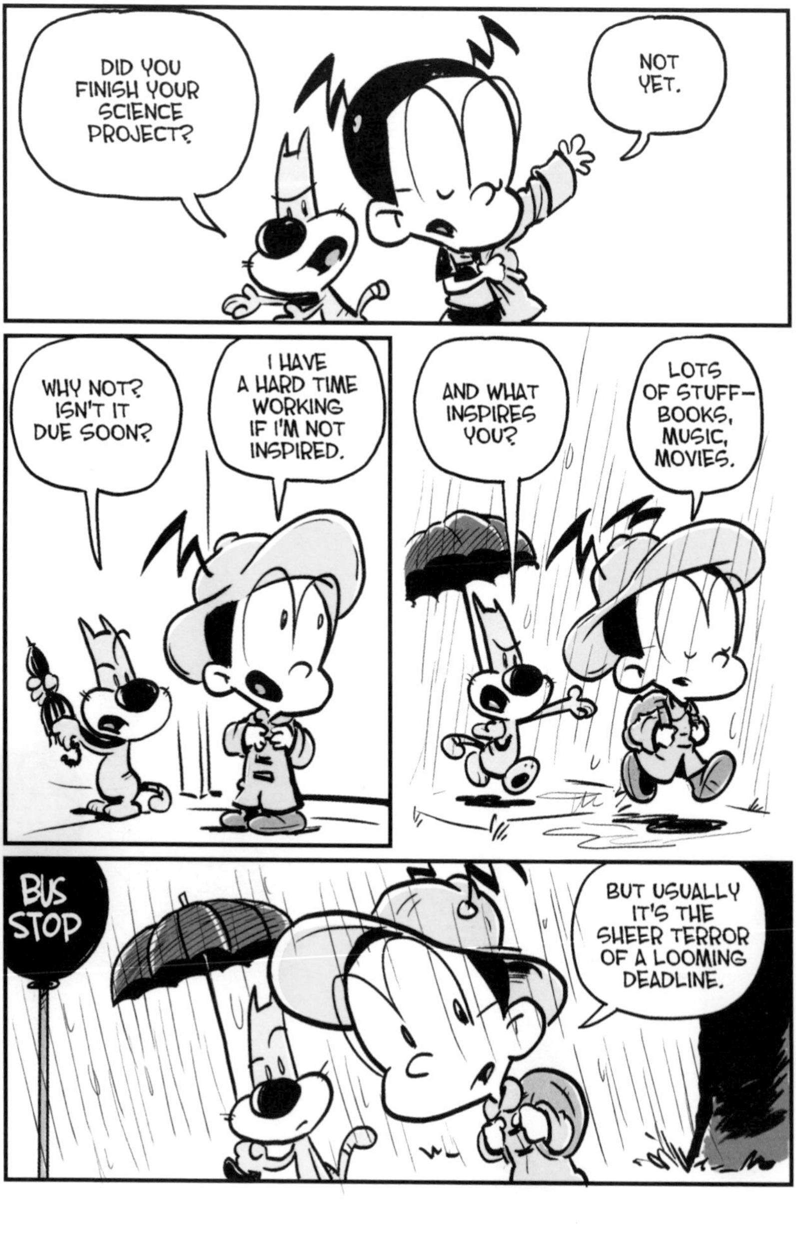
DID YOU FINISH YOUR SCIENCE PROJECT?
NOT YET.
WHY NOT? ISN'T IT DUE SOON?
I HAVE A HARD TIME WORKING IF I'M NOT INSPIRED.
AND WHAT INSPIRES YOU?
LOTS OF STUFF– BOOKS, MUSIC, MOVIES.
BUS STOP
BUT USUALLY IT'S THE SHEER TERROR OF A LOOMING DEADLINE.

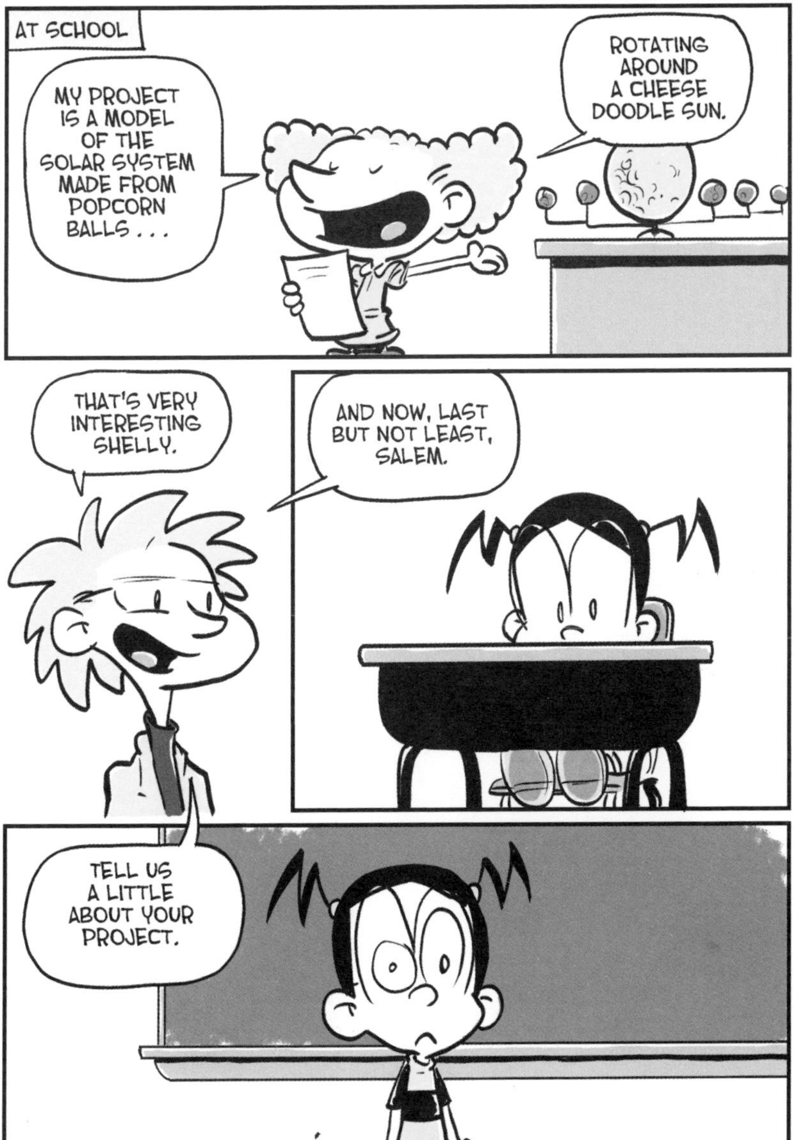
AT SCHOOL
MY PROJECT IS A MODEL OF THE SOLAR SYSTEM MADE FROM POPCORN BALLS . . .
ROTATING AROUND A CHEESE DOODLE SUN.
THAT'S VERY INTERESTING SHELLY.
AND NOW, LAST BUT NOT LEAST, SALEM.
TELL US A LITTLE ABOUT YOUR PROJECT.

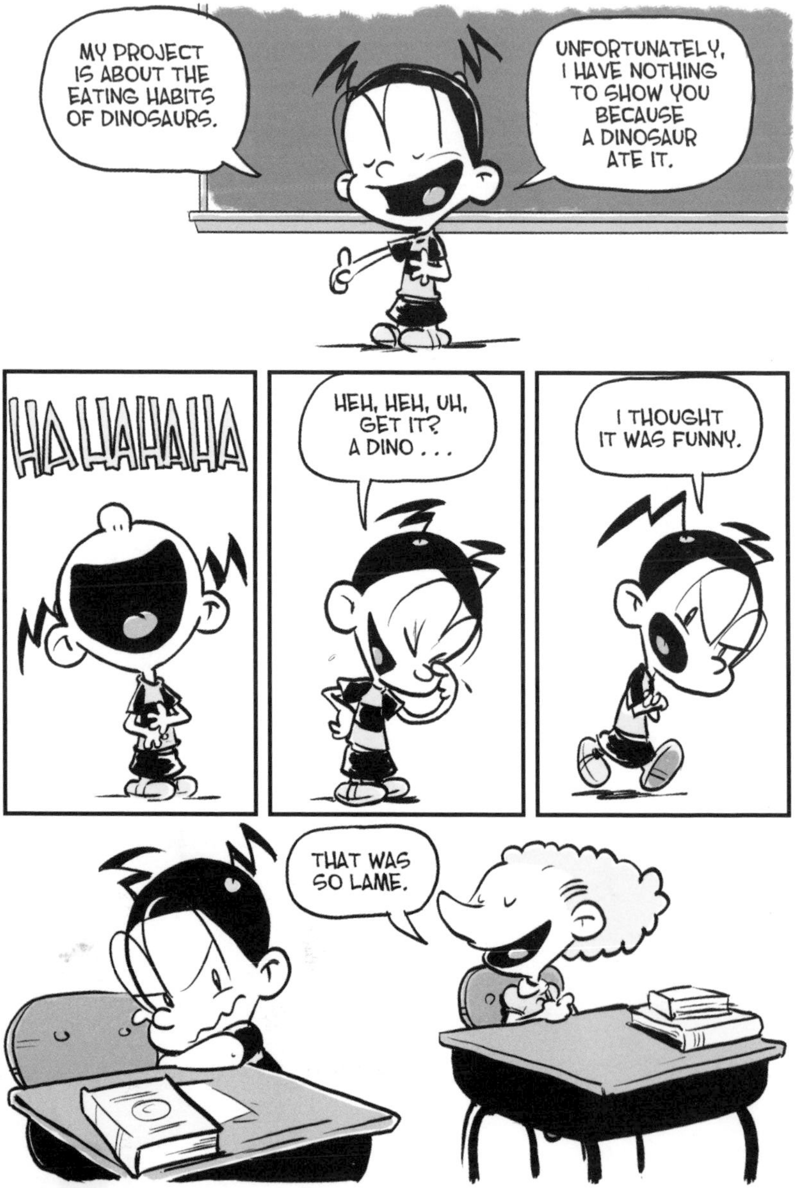
MY PROJECT IS ABOUT THE EATING HABITS OF DINOSAURS.
UNFORTUNATELY, I HAVE NOTHING TO SHOW YOU BECAUSE A DINOSAUR ATE IT.
HAHAHAHA
HEH, HEH, UH, GET IT? A DINO . . .
I THOUGHT IT WAS FUNNY.
THAT WAS SO LAME.

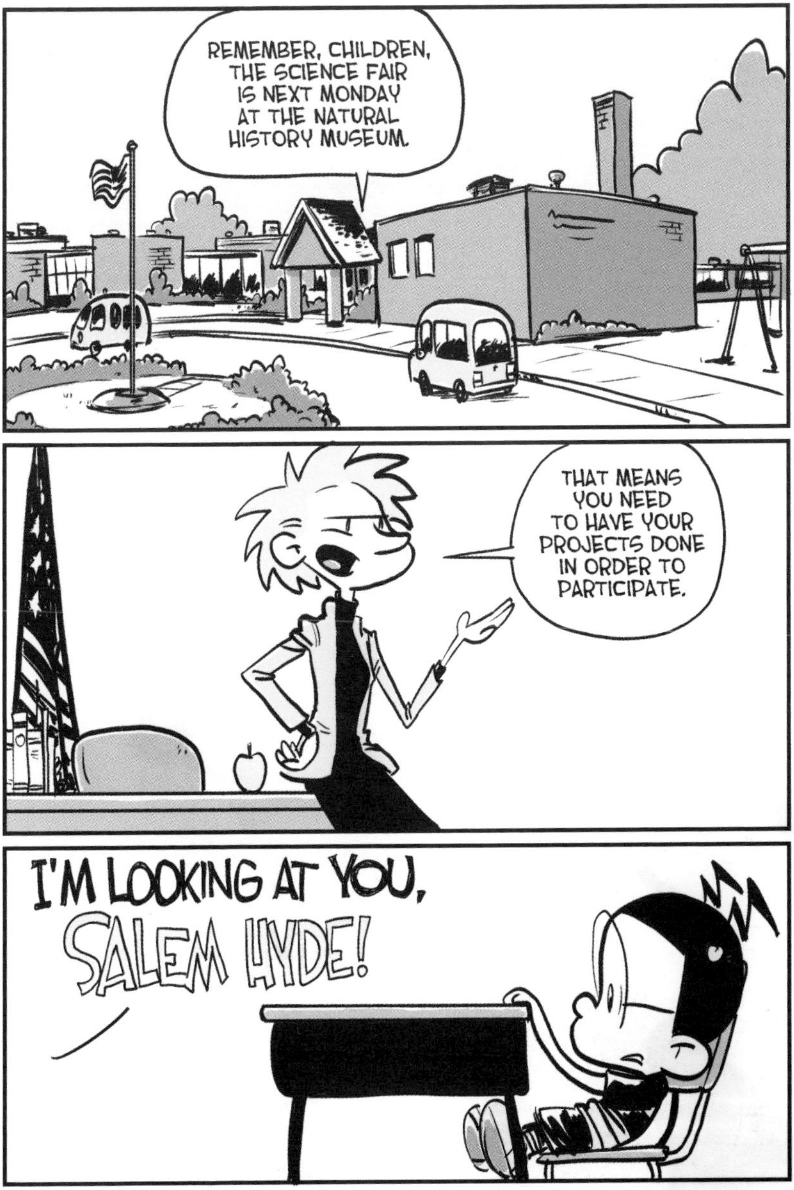
REMEMBER, CHILDREN, THE SCIENCE FAIR IS NEXT MONDAY AT THE NATURAL HISTORY MUSEUM.
THAT MEANS YOU NEED TO HAVE YOUR PROJECTS DONE IN ORDER TO PARTICIPATE.
I'M LOOKING AT YOU, SALEM HYDE!

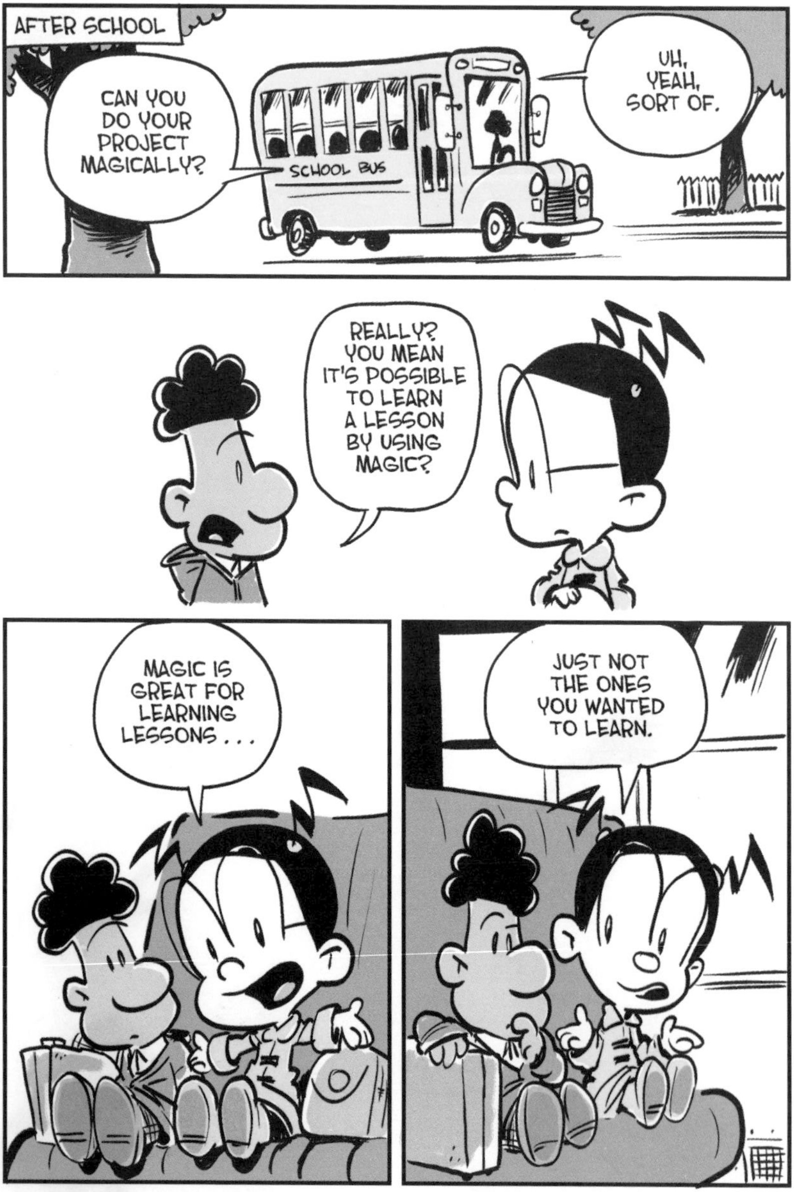
AFTER SCHOOL
CAN YOU DO YOUR PROJECT MAGICALLY?
SCHOOL BUS
UH, YEAH, SORT OF.
REALLY? YOU MEAN IT'S POSSIBLE TO LEARN A LESSON BY USING MAGIC?
MAGIC IS GREAT FOR LEARNING LESSONS . . .
JUST NOT THE ONES YOU WANTED TO LEARN.

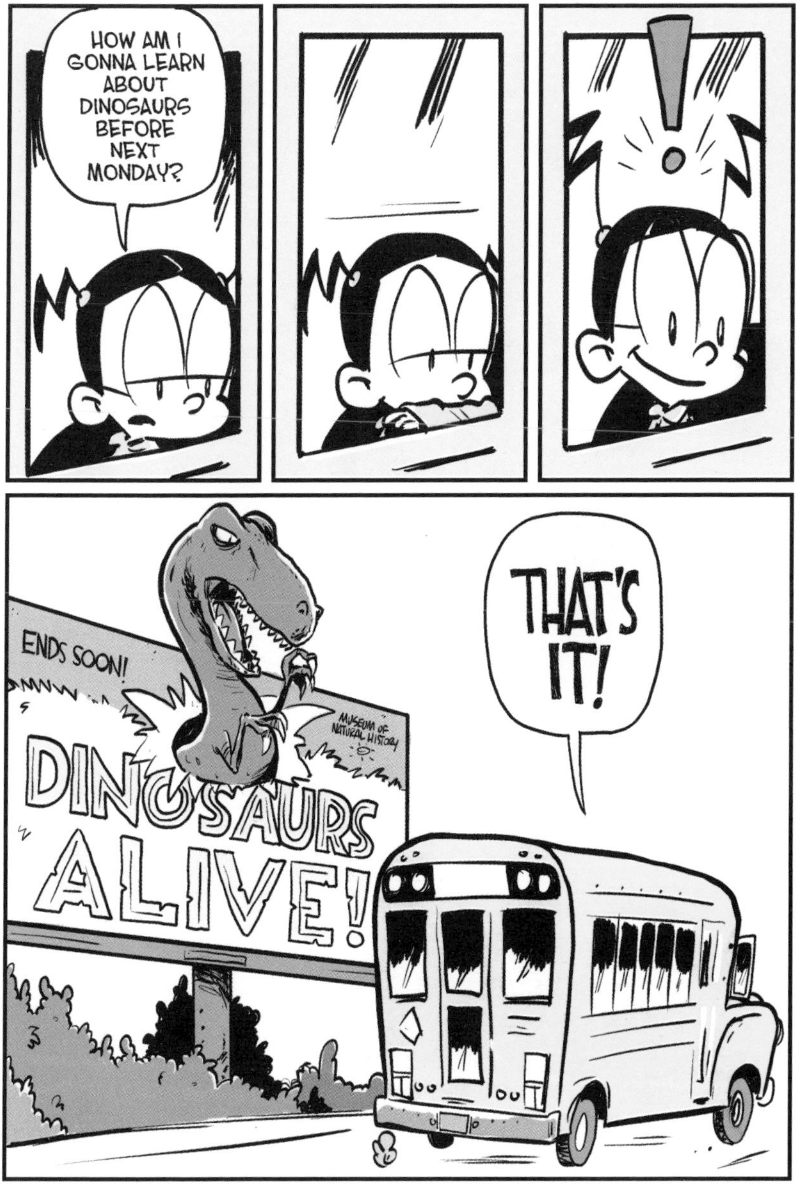
HOW AM I GONNA LEARN ABOUT DINOSAURS BEFORE NEXT MONDAY?
!
ENDS SOON!
MUSEUM OF NATURAL HISTORY
DINOSAURS ALIVE!
THAT'S IT!

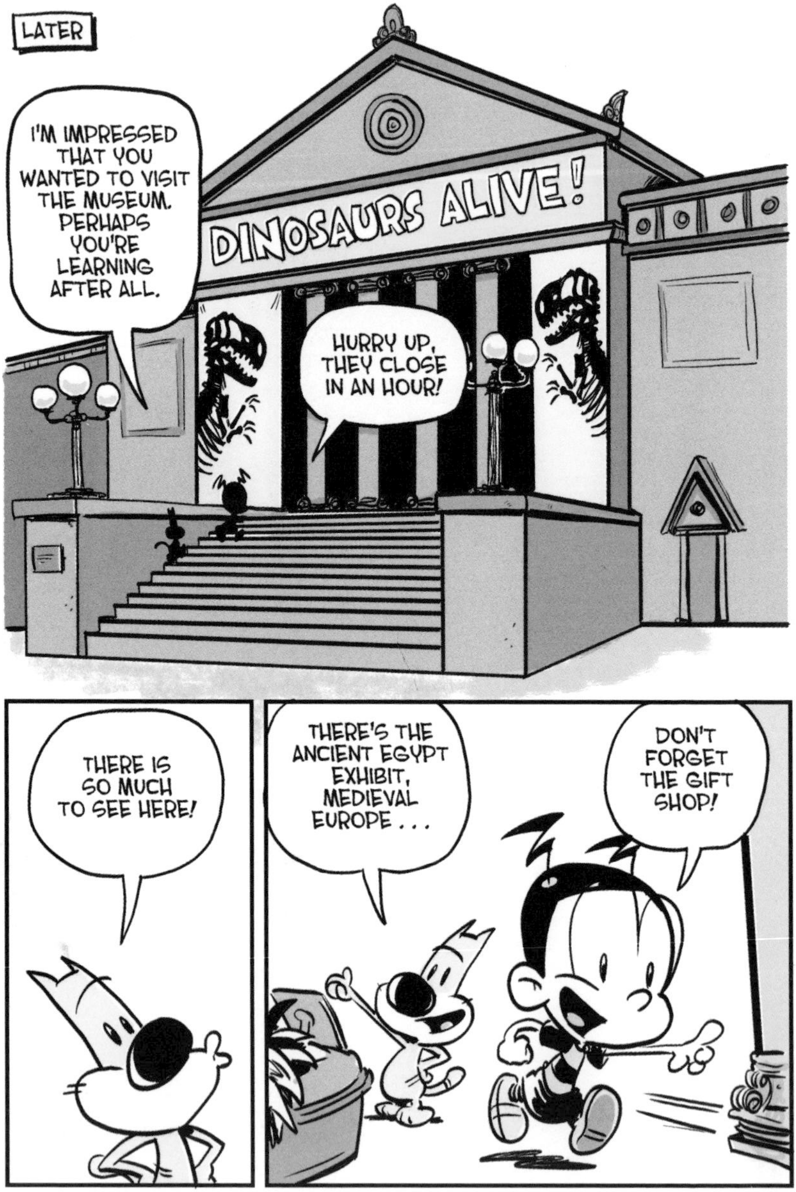
LATER
I'M IMPRESSED THAT YOU WANTED TO VISIT THE MUSEUM. PERHAPS YOU'RE LEARNING AFTER ALL.
DINOSAURS ALIVE!
HURRY UP, THEY CLOSE IN AN HOUR!
THERE IS SO MUCH TO SEE HERE!
THERE'S THE ANCIENT EGYPT EXHIBIT, MEDIEVAL EUROPE . . .
DON'T FORGET THE GIFT SHOP!

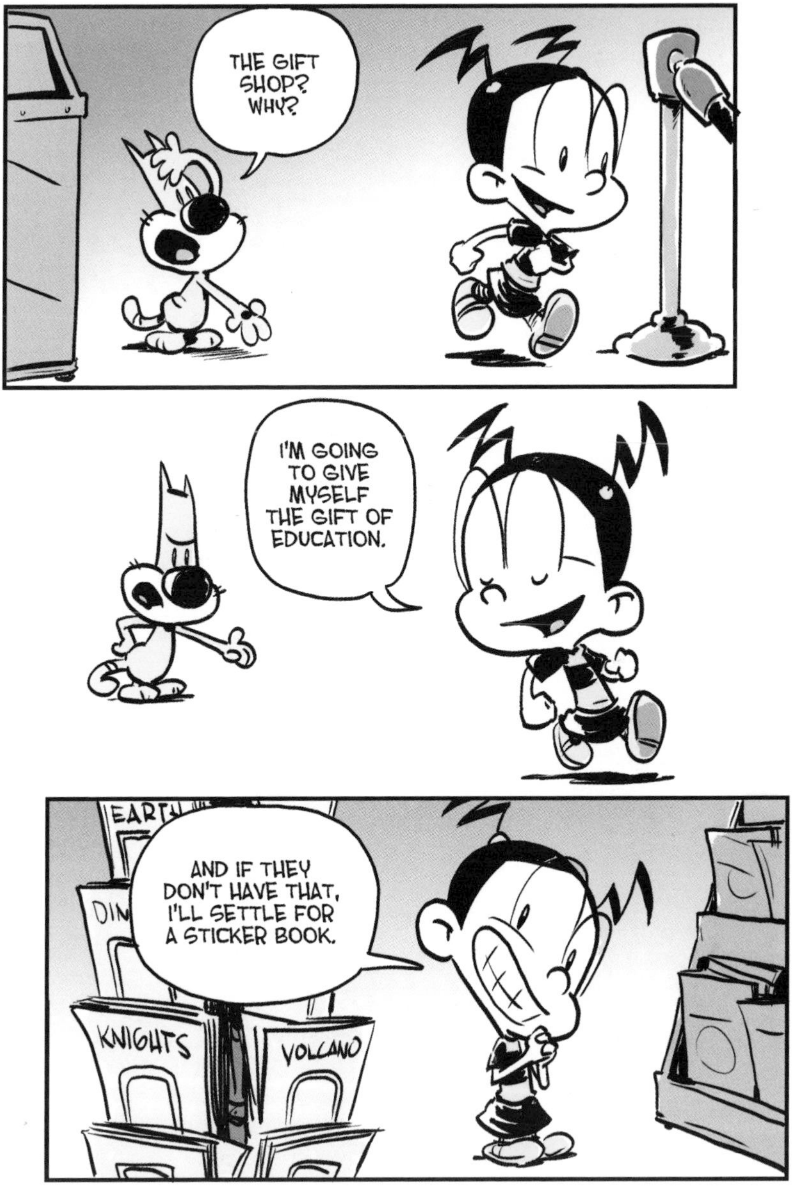
THE GIFT SHOP? WHY?
I'M GOING TO GIVE MYSELF THE GIFT OF EDUCATION.
AND IF THEY DON'T HAVE THAT, I'LL SETTLE FOR A STICKER BOOK.
KNIGHTS
VOLCANO

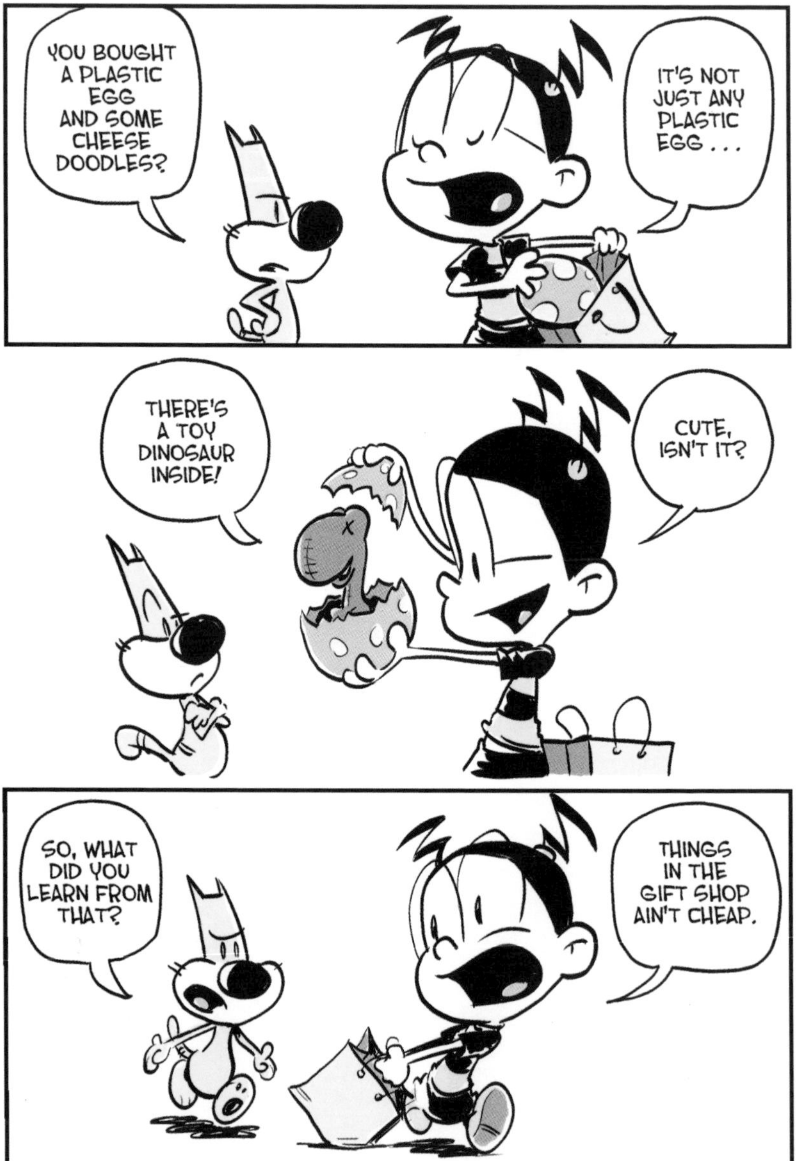
YOU BOUGHT A PLASTIC EGG AND SOME CHEESE DOODLES?
IT'S NOT JUST ANY PLASTIC EGG . . .
THERE'S A TOY DINOSAUR INSIDE!
CUTE, ISN'T IT?
SO, WHAT DID YOU LEARN FROM THAT?
THINGS IN THE GIFT SHOP AIN'T CHEAP.

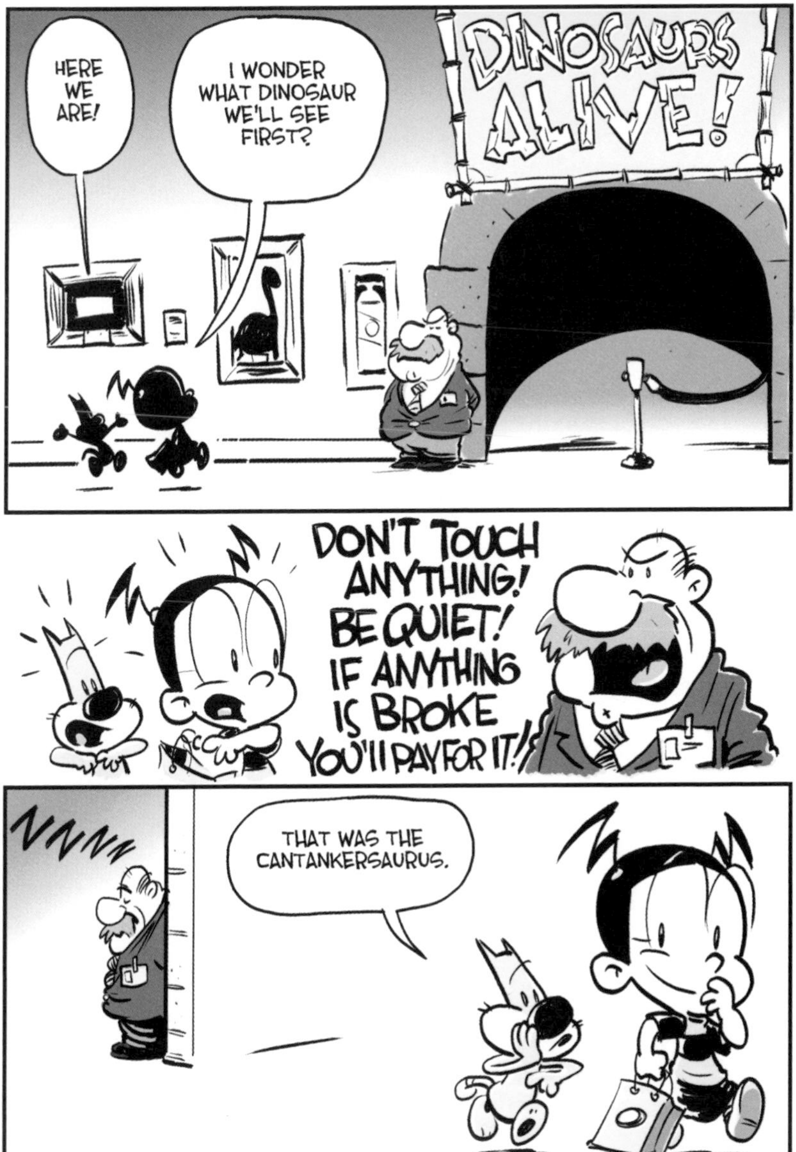
HERE WE ARE!
I WONDER WHAT DINOSAUR WE'LL SEE FIRST?
DINOSAURS ALIVE!
DON'T TOUCH ANYTHING! BE QUIET! IF ANYTHING IS BROKE YOU'll PAY FOR IT!
NNNN
THAT WAS THE CANTANKERSAURUS.

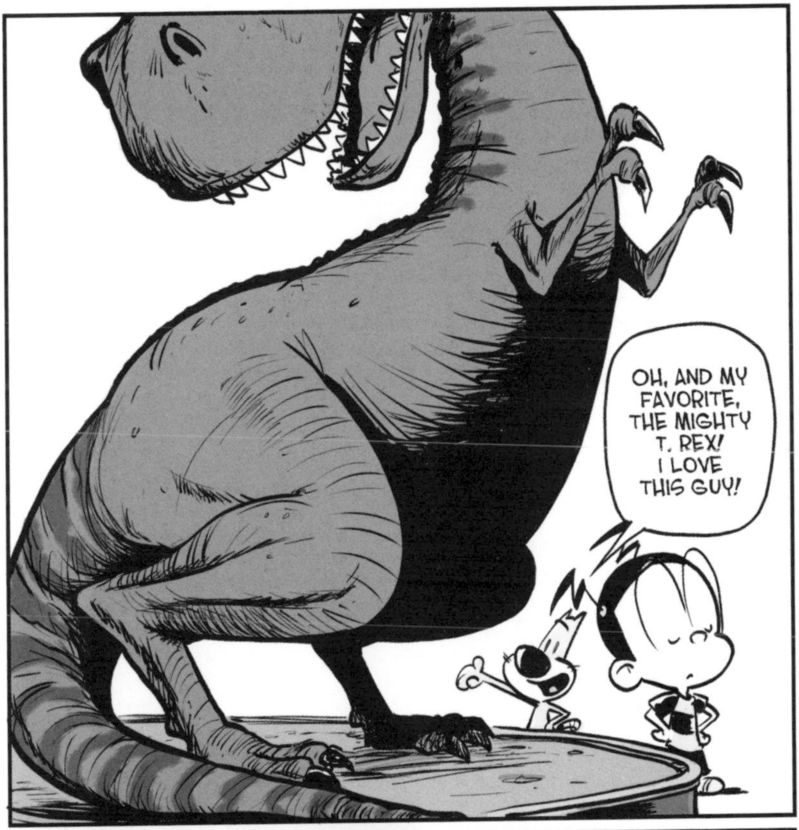
OH, AND MY FAVORITE, THE MIGHTY T. REX! I LOVE THIS GUY!

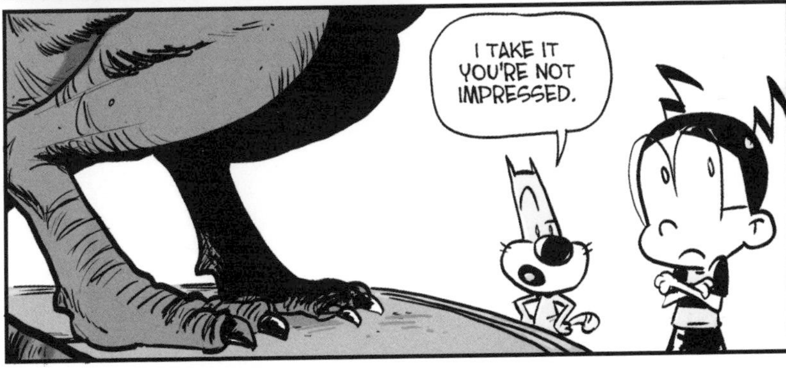
I TAKE IT YOU'RE NOT IMPRESSED.

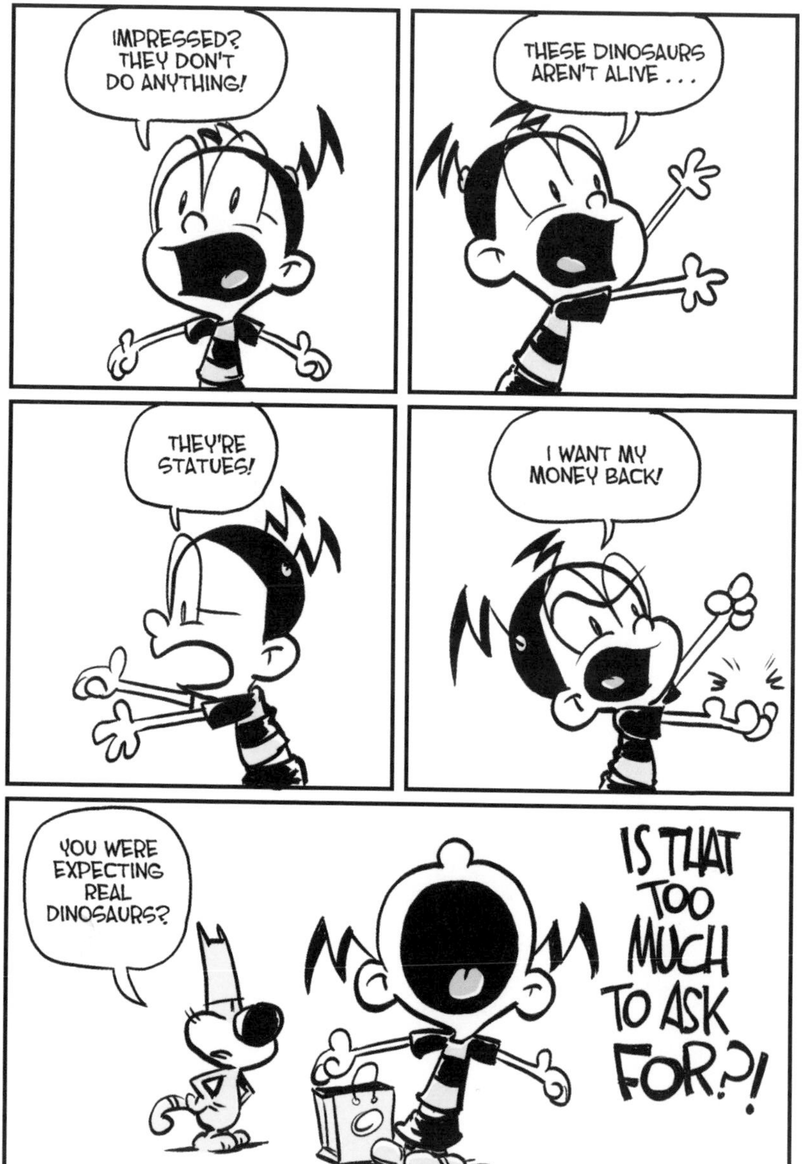

IMPRESSED? THEY DON'T DO ANYTHING!
THESE DINOSAURS AREN'T ALIVE . . .
THEY'RE STATUES!
I WANT MY MONEY BACK!
YOU WERE EXPECTING REAL DINOSAURS?
IS THAT TOO MUCH TO ASK FOR?!

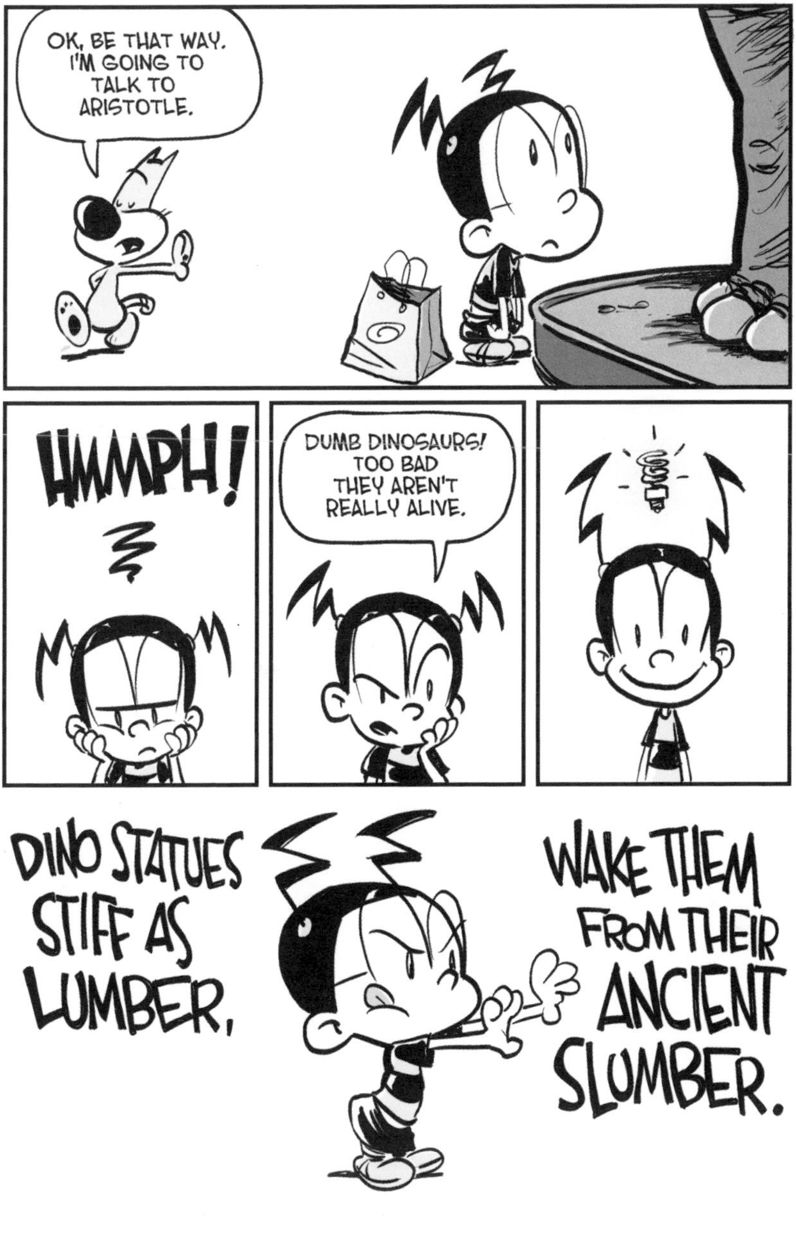
OK, BE THAT WAY. I'M GOING TO TALK TO ARISTOTLE.
HMMPH!
DUMB DINOSAURS! TOO BAD THEY AREN'T REALLY ALIVE.
DINO STATUES STIFF AS LUMBER,
WAKE THEM FROM THEIR ANCIENT SLUMBER.

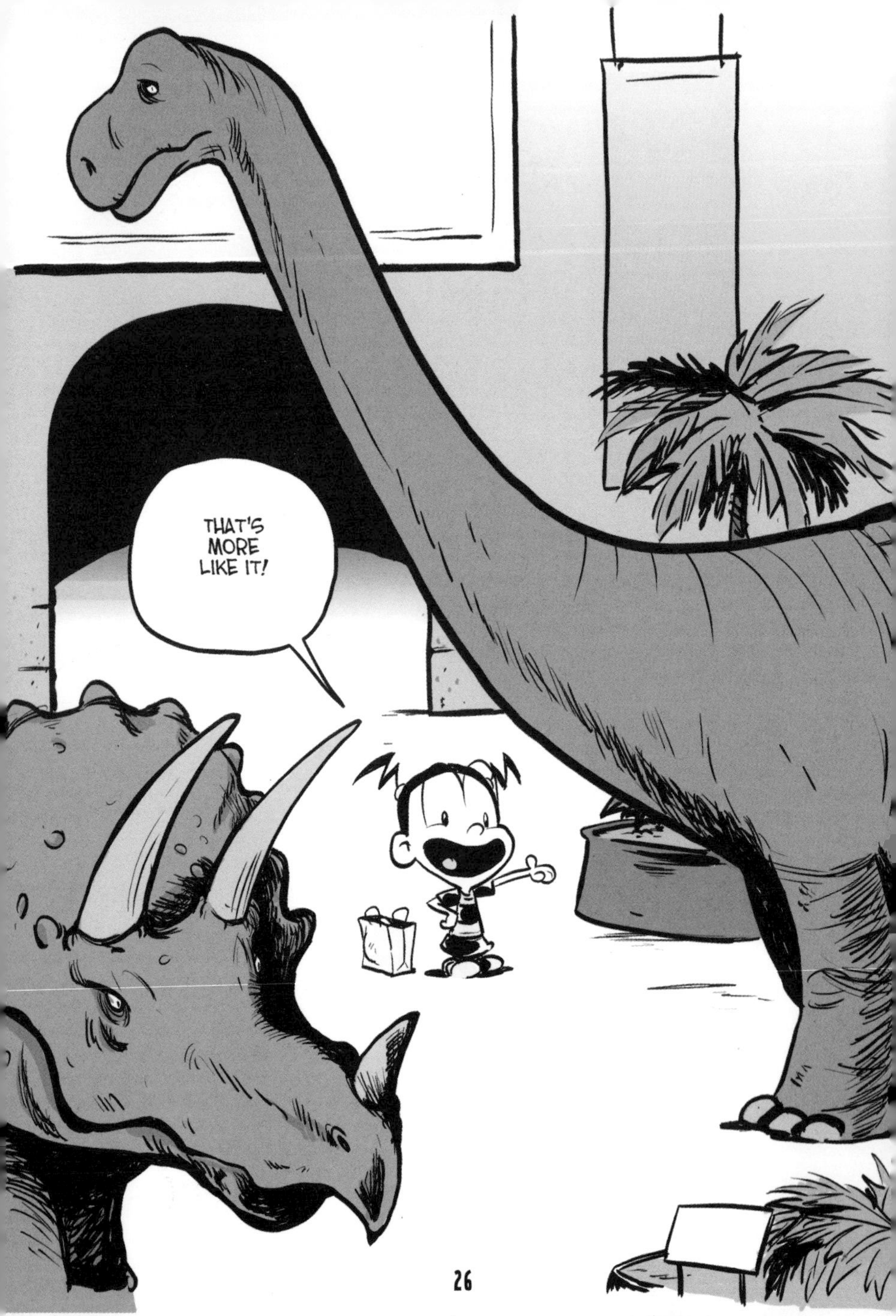
THAT'S MORE LIKE IT!

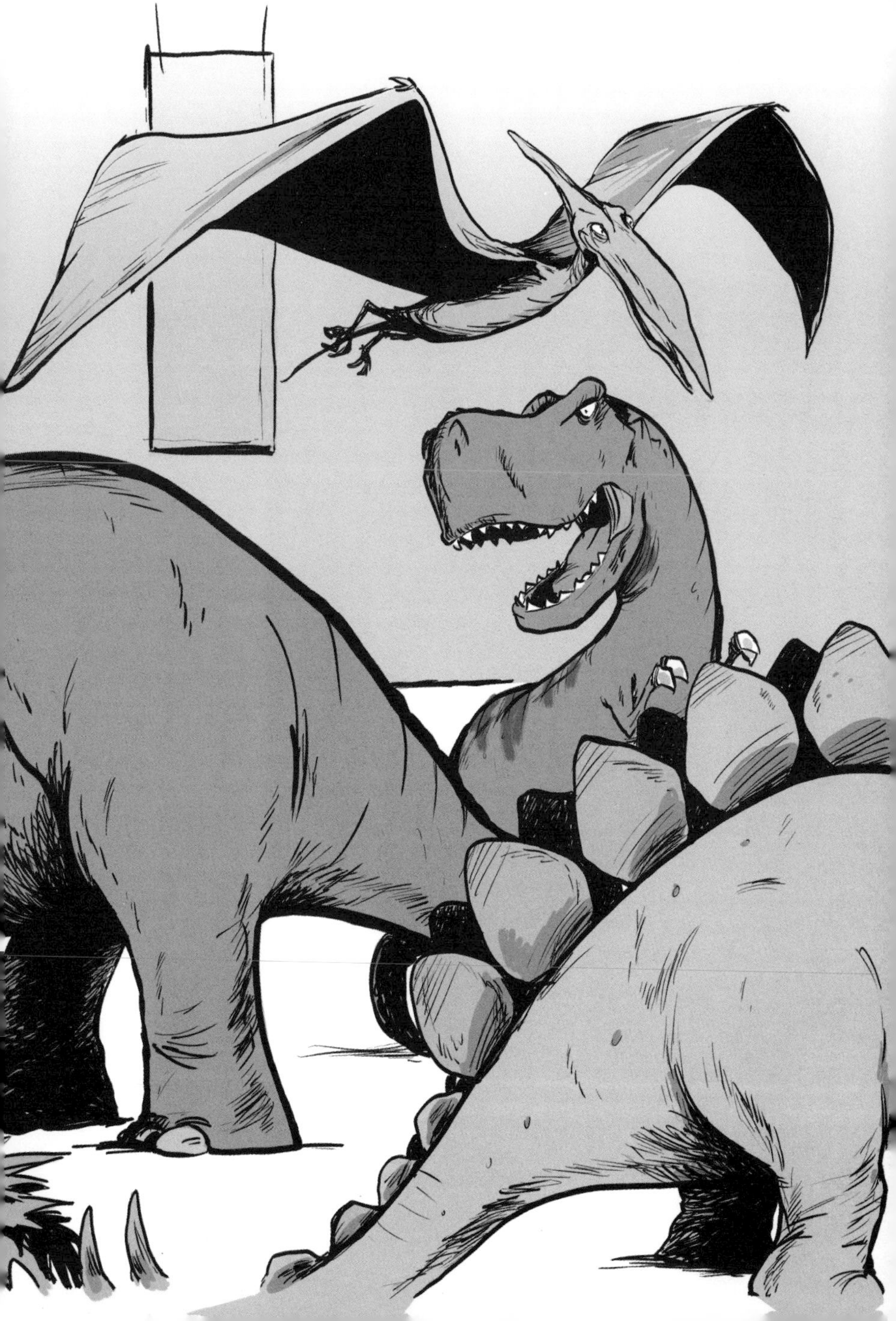

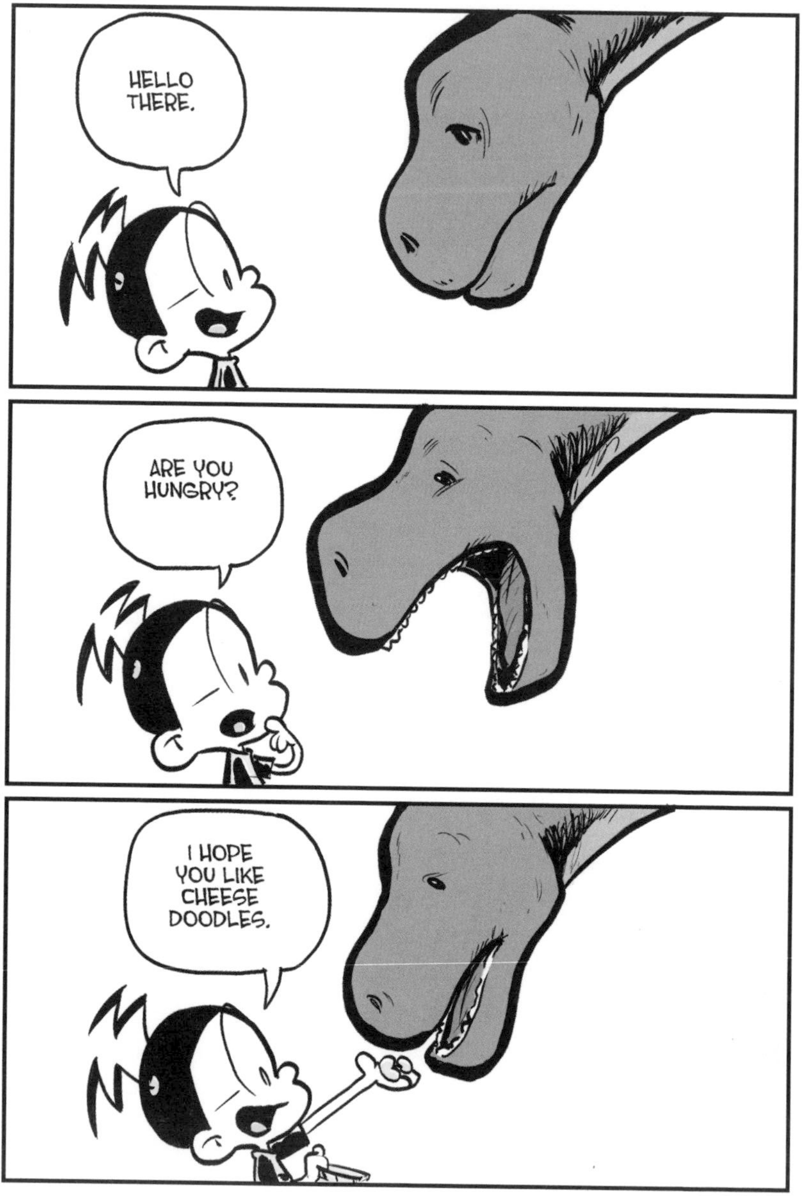
HELLO THERE.
ARE YOU HUNGRY?
I HOPE YOU LIKE CHEESE DOODLES.

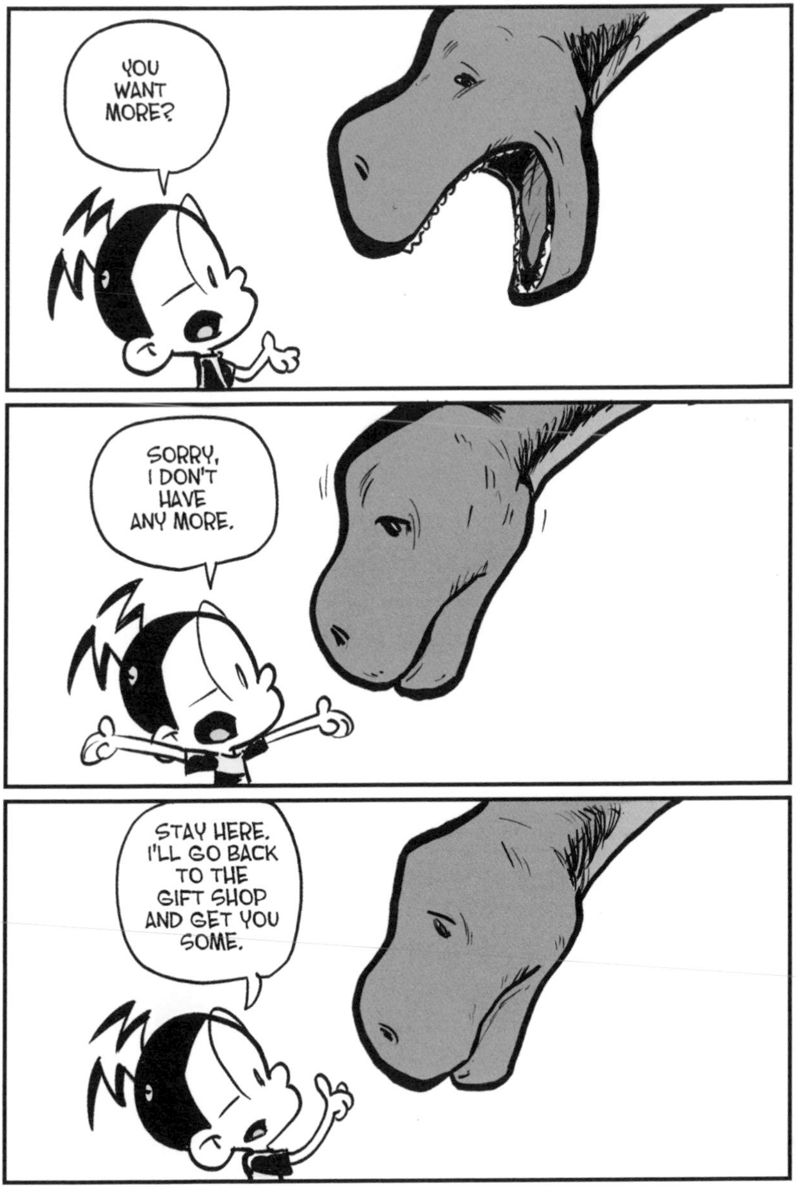
YOU WANT MORE?
SORRY, I DON'T HAVE ANY MORE.
STAY HERE. I'LL GO BACK TO THE GIFT SHOP AND GET YOU SOME.

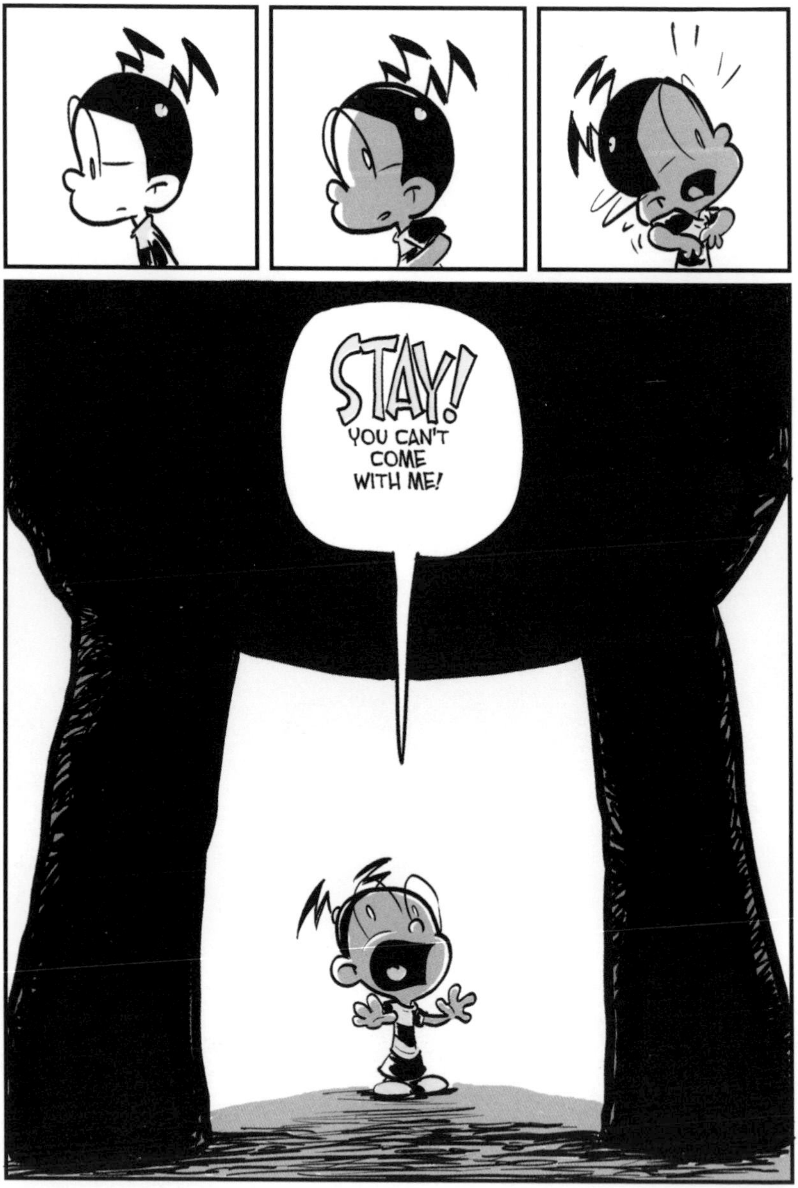
STAY!
YOU CAN'T COME WITH ME!

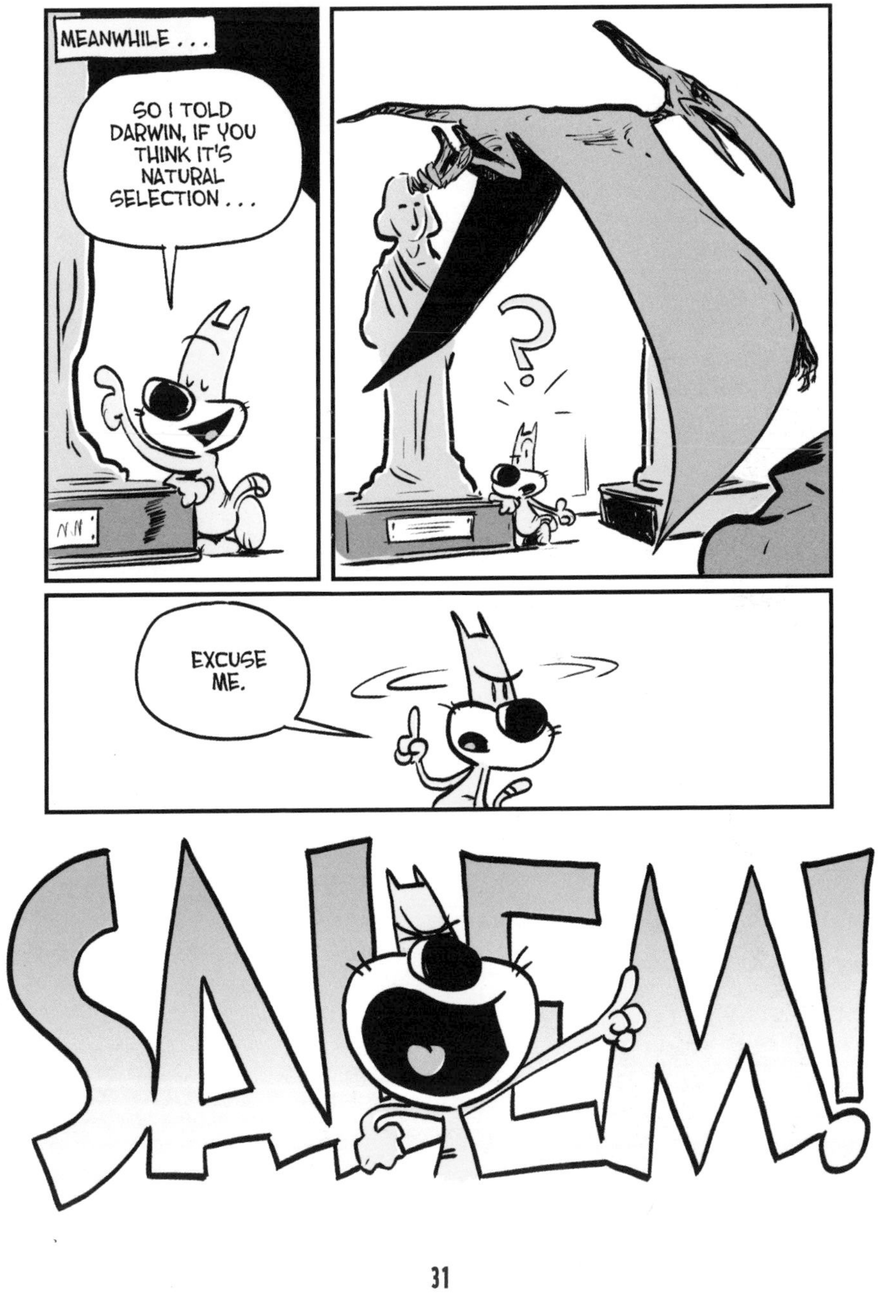
MEANWHILE . . .
SO I TOLD DARWIN, IF YOU THINK IT'S NATURAL SELECTION . . .
?
EXCUSE ME.
SALEM!

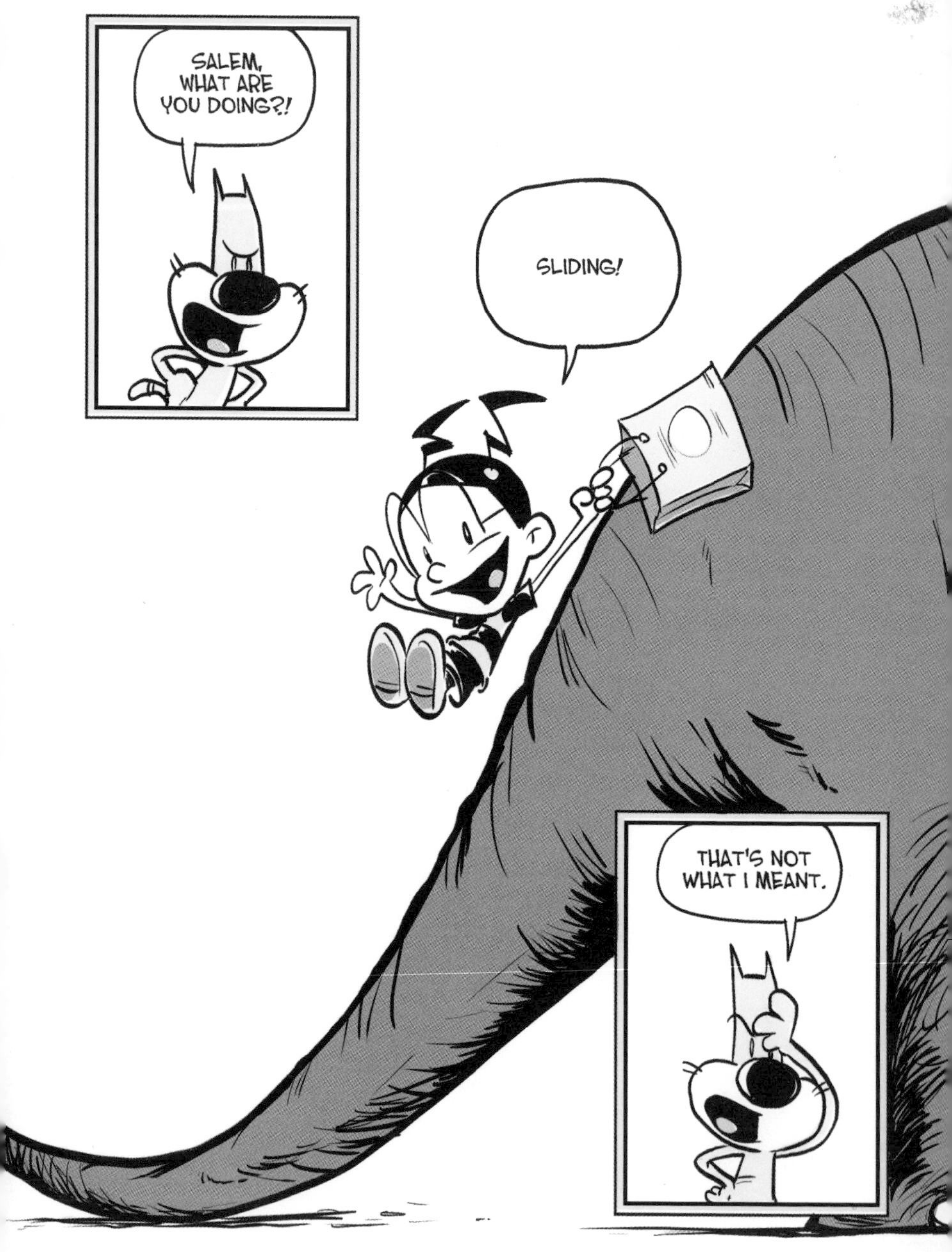
SALEM, WHAT ARE YOU DOING?!
SLIDING!
THAT'S NOT WHAT I MEANT.

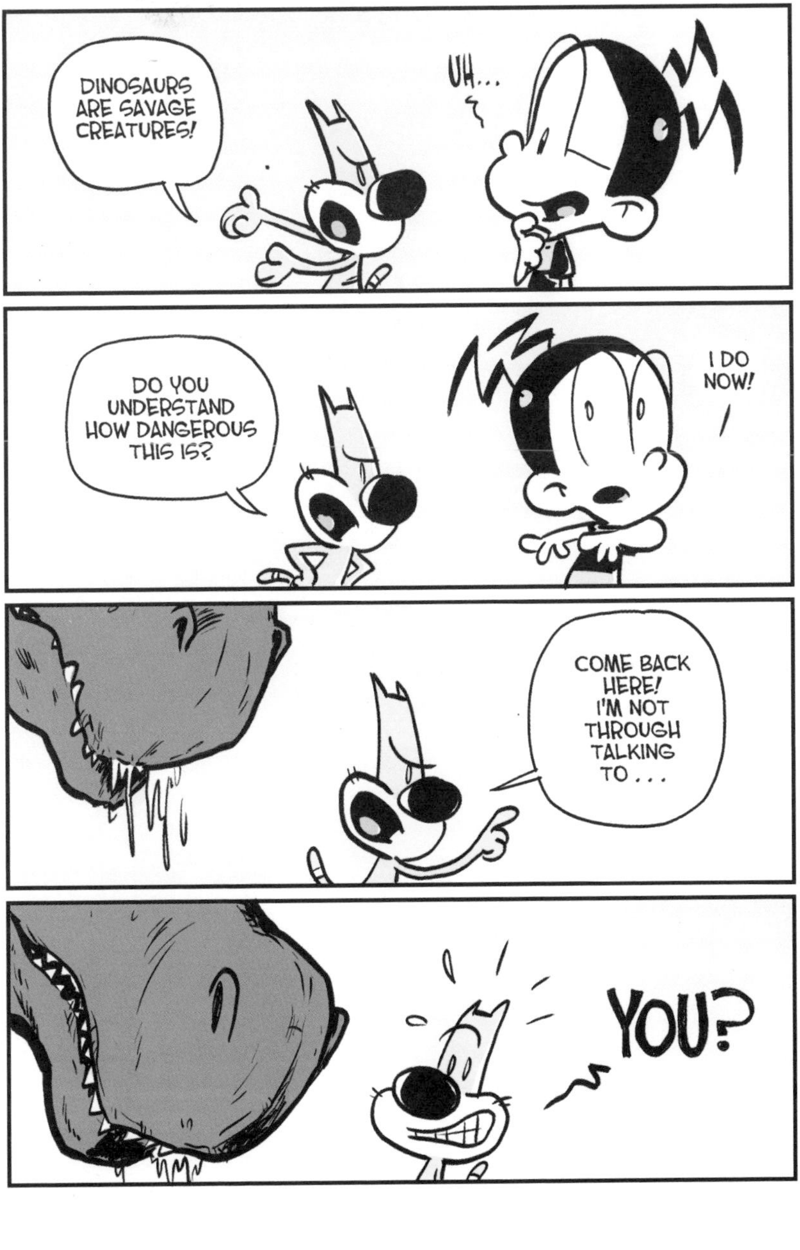
DINOSAURS ARE SAVAGE CREATURES!
UH...
DO YOU UNDERSTAND HOW DANGEROUS THIS IS?
I DO NOW!
COME BACK HERE! I'M NOT THROUGH TALKING TO . . .
YOU?

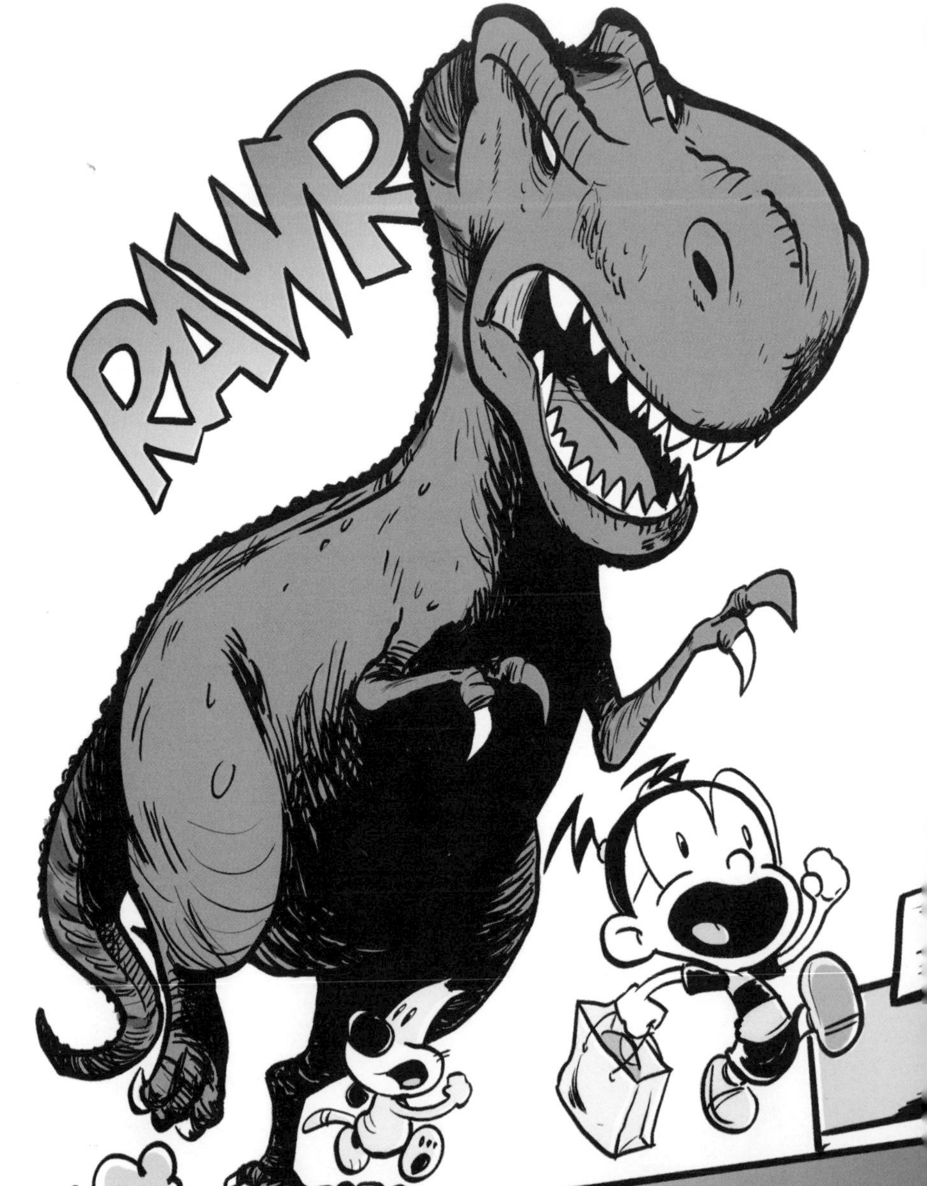
RAWR

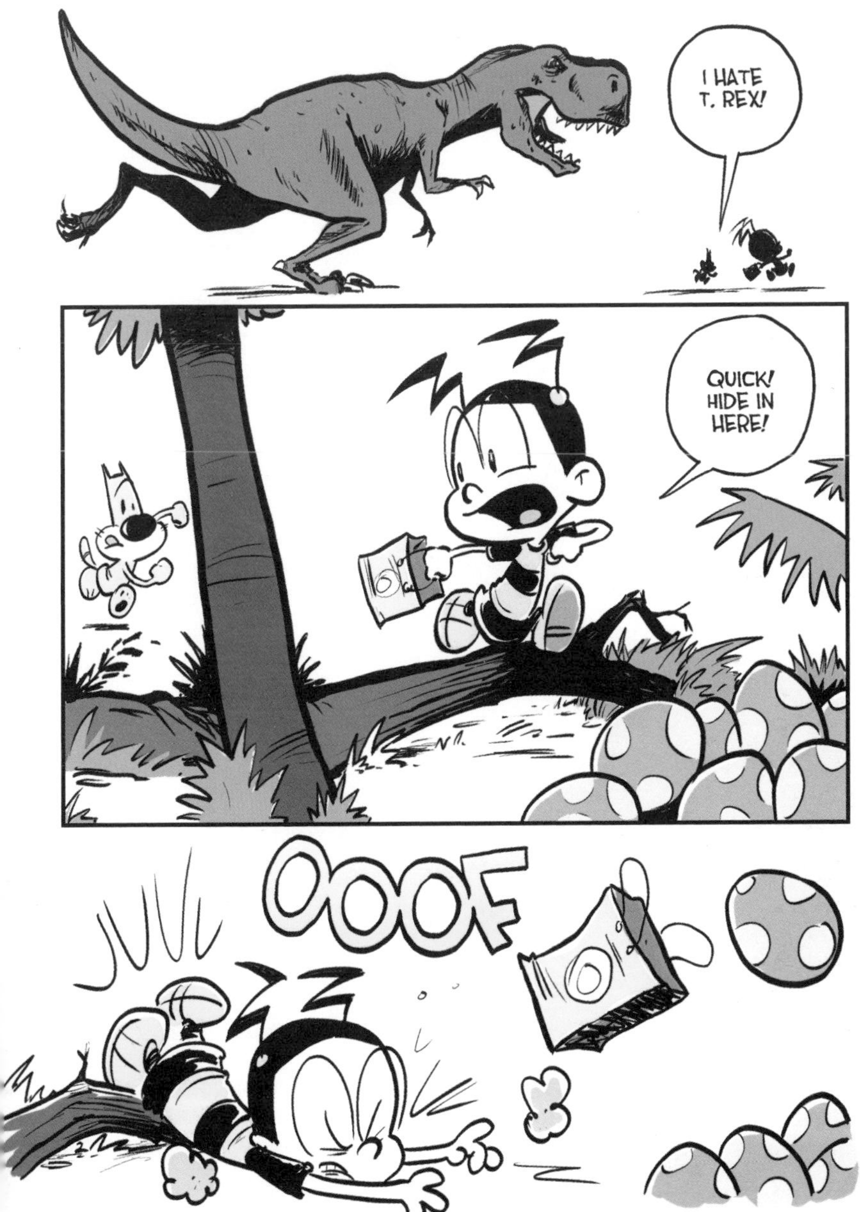
I HATE T. REX!
QUICK! HIDE IN HERE!
OOOF

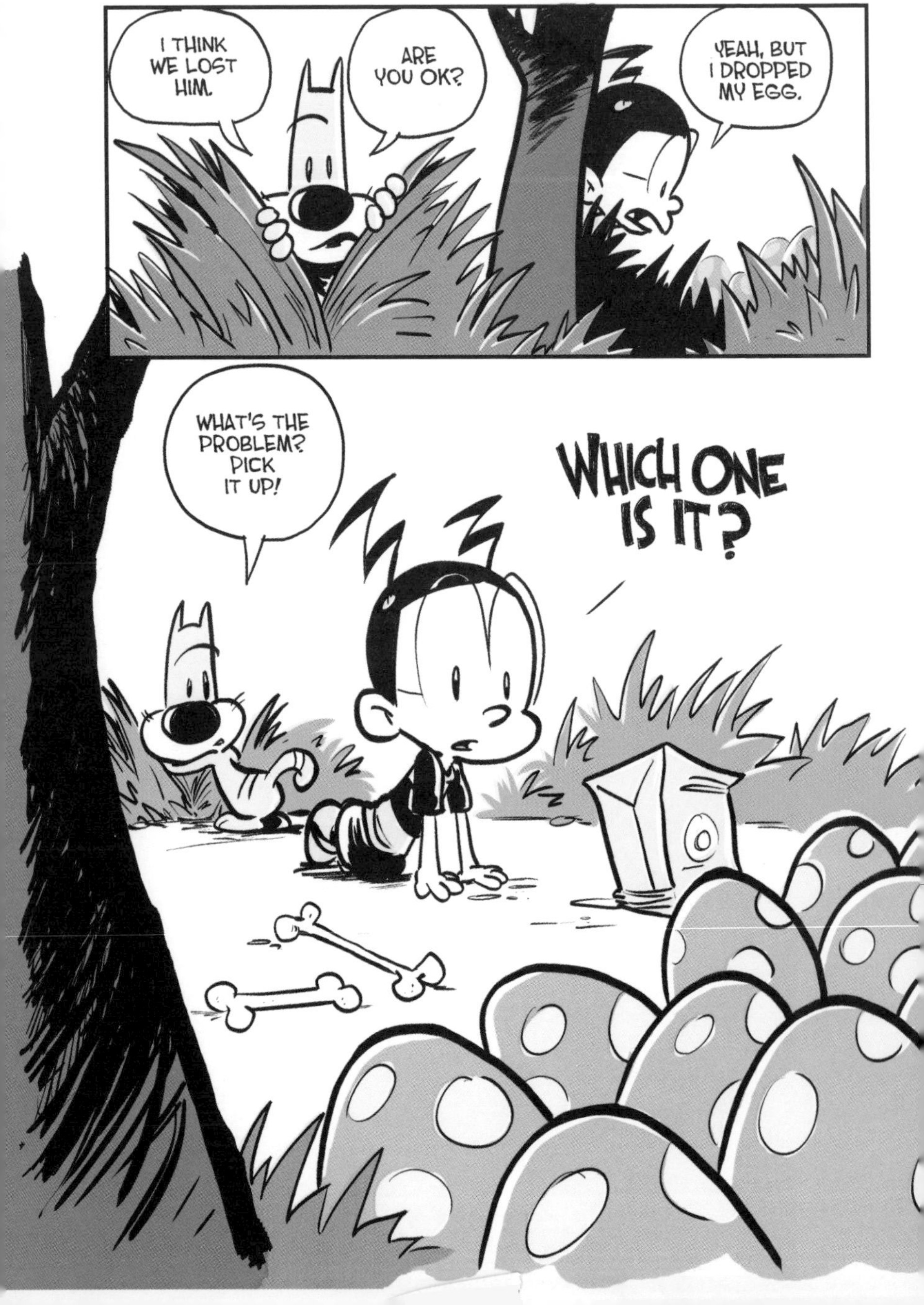
I THINK WE LOST HIM.
ARE YOU OK?
YEAH, BUT I DROPPED MY EGG.
WHAT'S THE PROBLEM? PICK IT UP!
WHICH ONE IS IT?

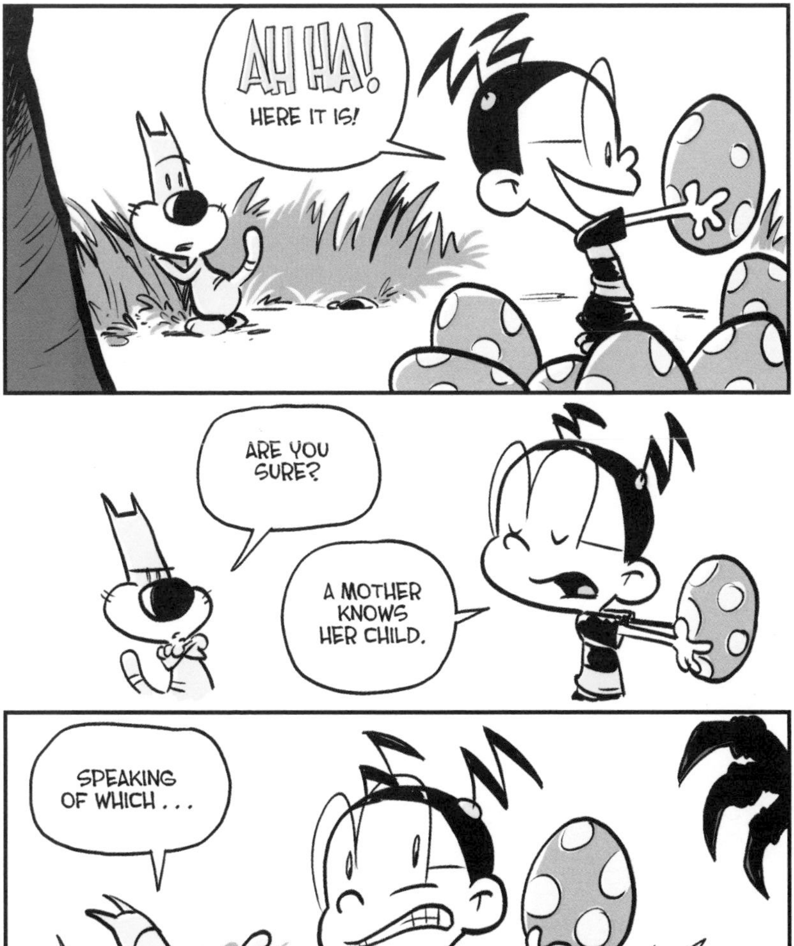
AH HA!
HERE IT IS!
ARE YOU SURE?
A MOTHER KNOWS HER CHILD.
SPEAKING OF WHICH . . .

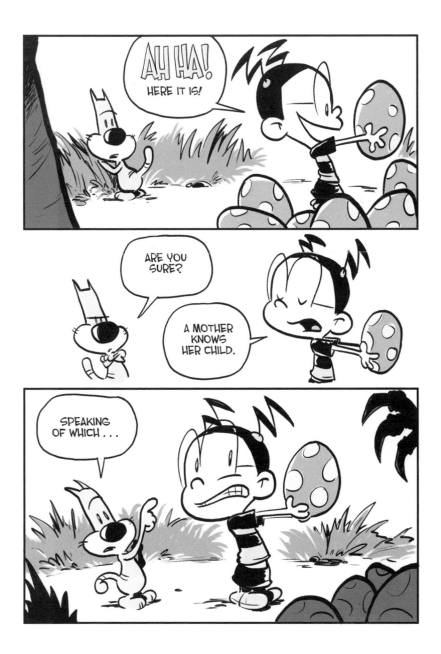

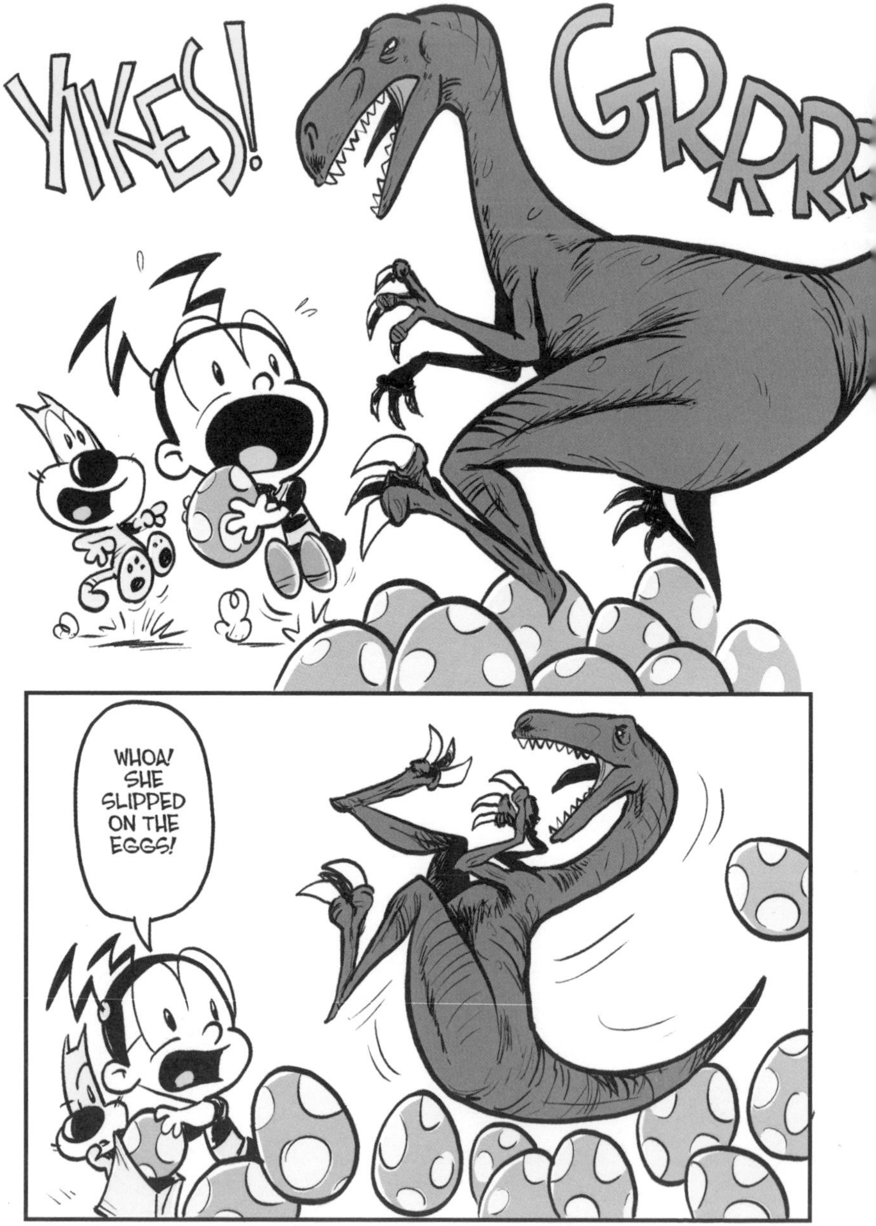
YIKES!
GRRRR
WHOA! SHE SLIPPED ON THE EGGS!

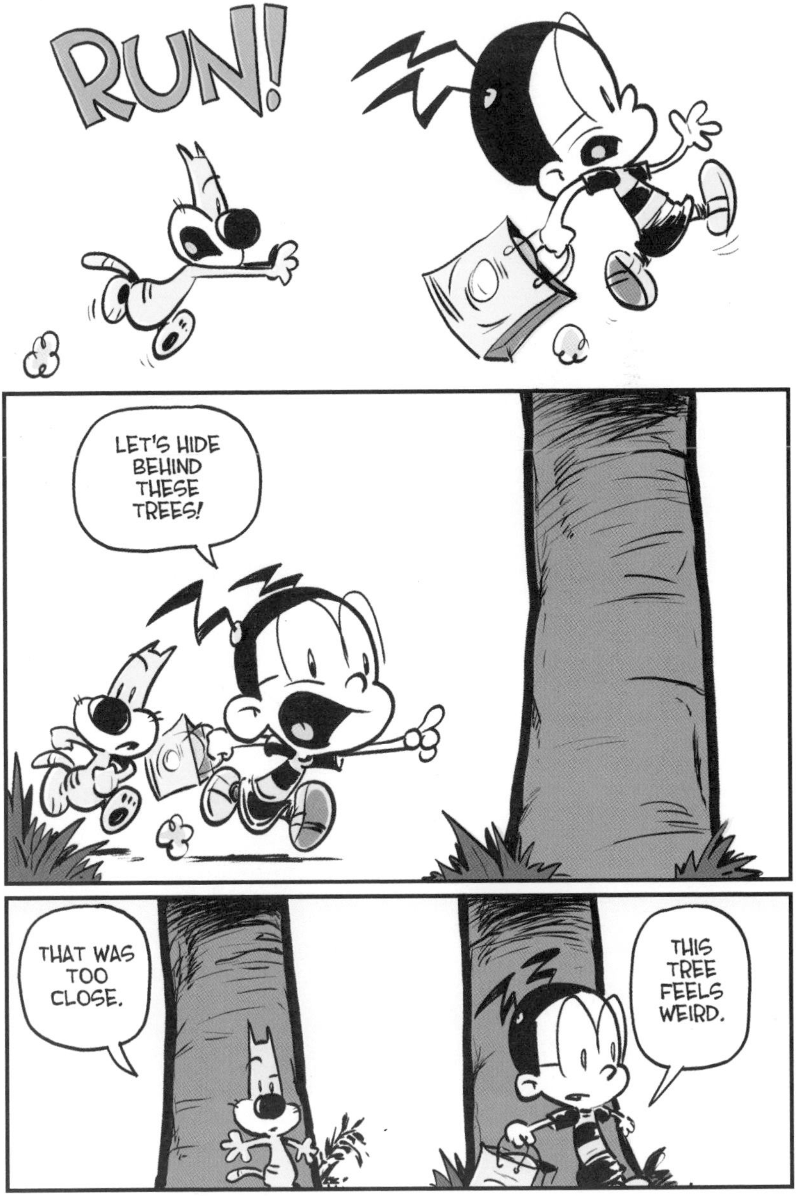
RUN!
LET'S HIDE BEHIND THESE TREES!
THAT WAS TOO CLOSE.
THIS TREE FEELS WEIRD.

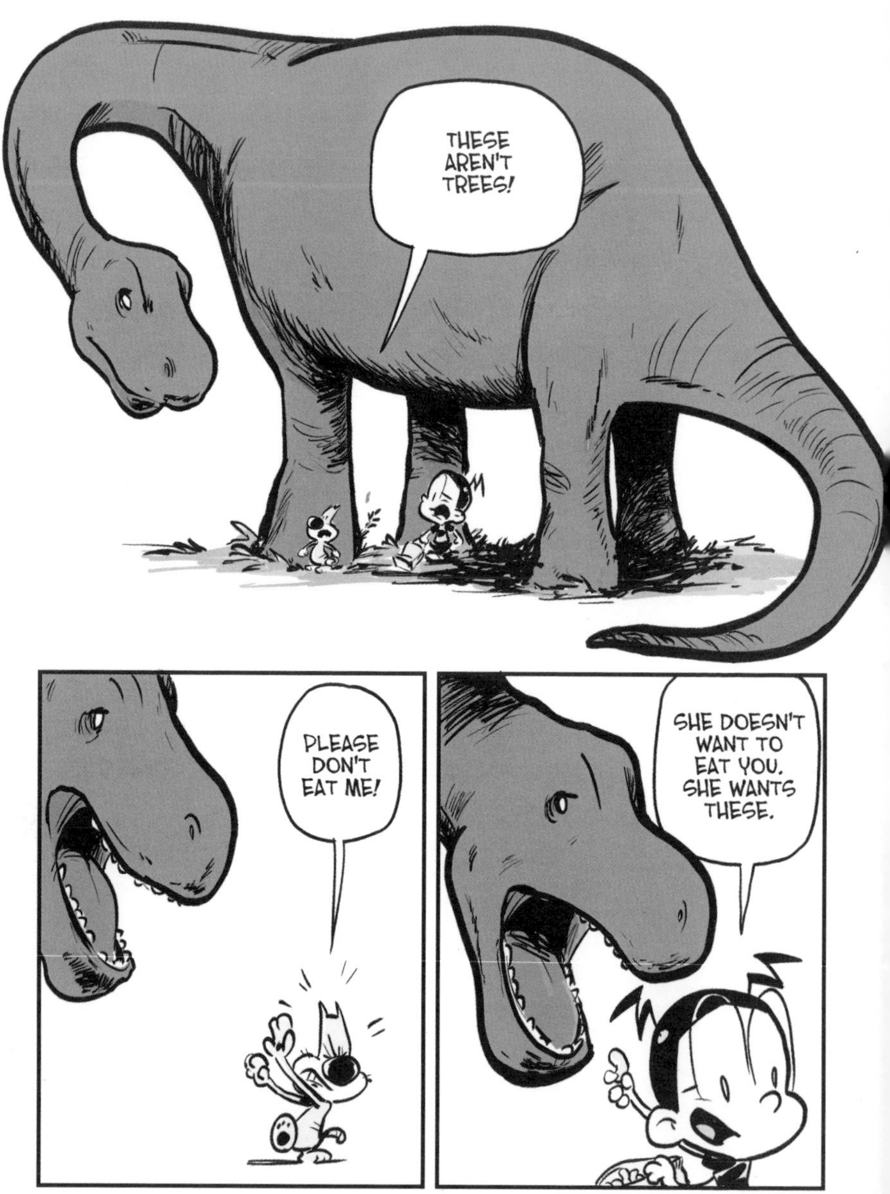
THESE AREN'T TREES!
PLEASE DON'T EAT ME!
SHE DOESN'T WANT TO EAT YOU. SHE WANTS THESE.

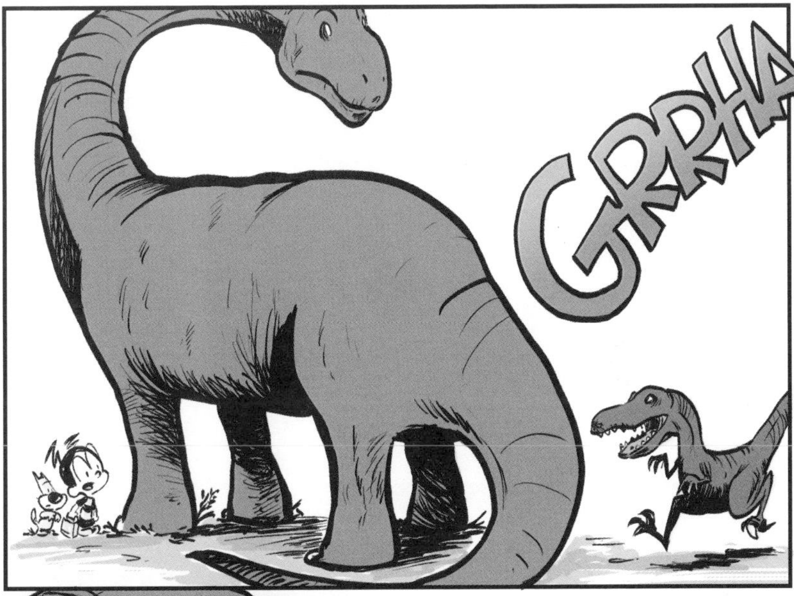
GRRHA

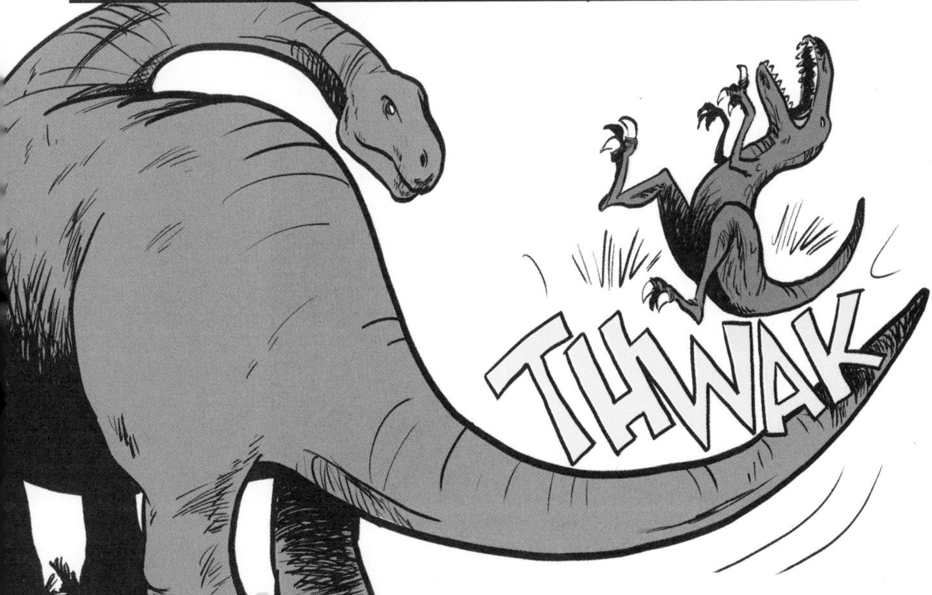
THWAK

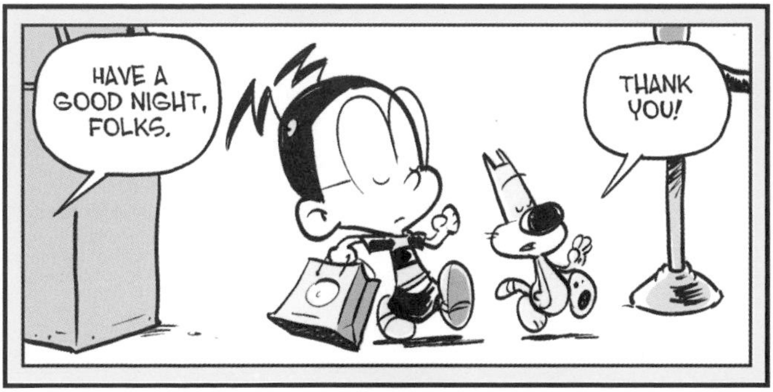
HAVE A GOOD NIGHT, FOLKS.
THANK YOU!

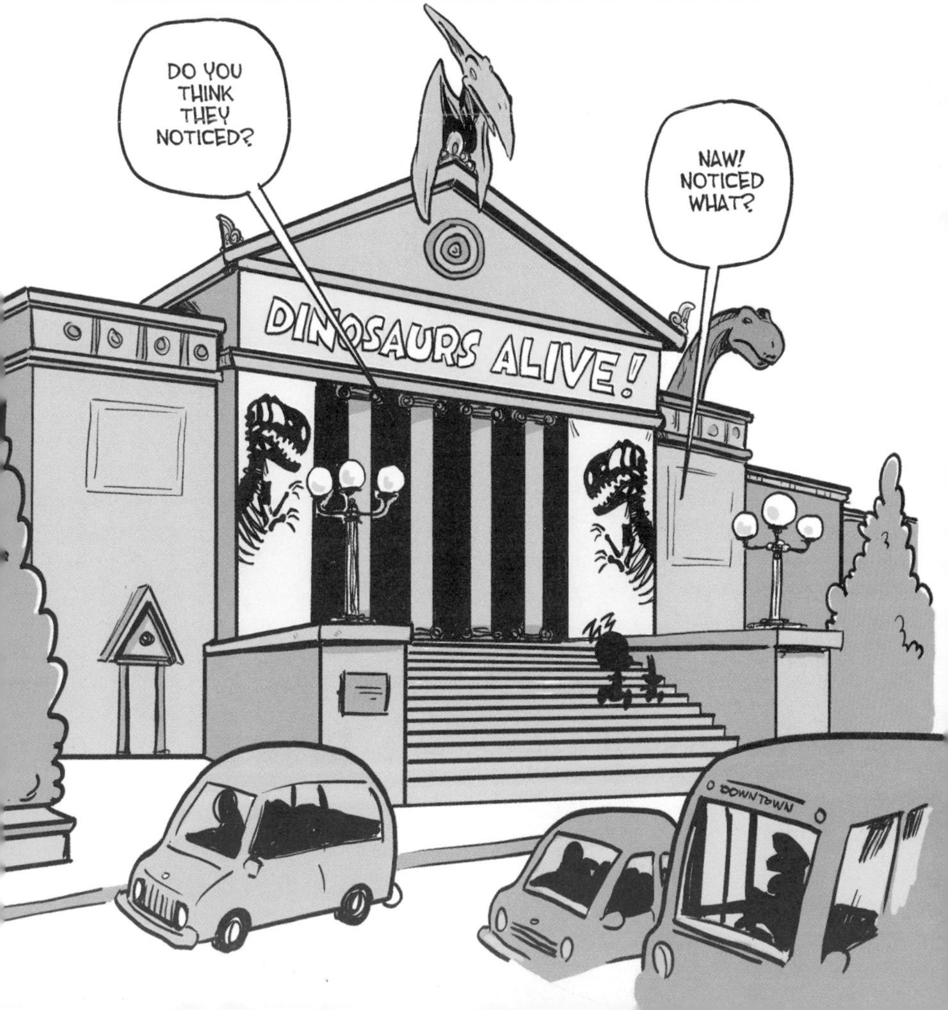
DO YOU THINK THEY NOTICED?
NAW! NOTICED WHAT?
DINOSAURS ALIVE!
DOWNTOWN

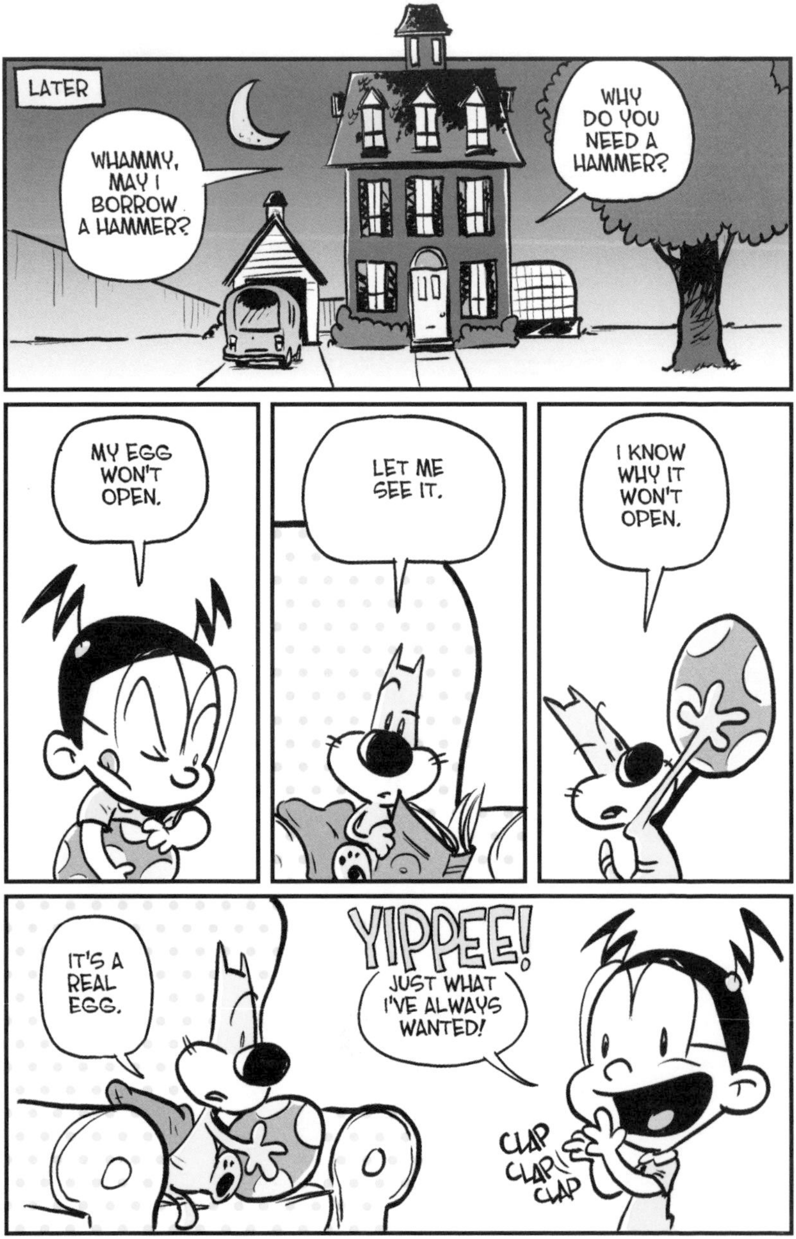
LATER
WHAMMY, MAY I BORROW A HAMMER?
WHY DO YOU NEED A HAMMER?
MY EGG WON'T OPEN.
LET ME SEE IT.
I KNOW WHY IT WON'T OPEN.
IT'S A REAL EGG.
YIPPEE!
JUST WHAT I'VE ALWAYS WANTED!
CLAP CLAP CLAP

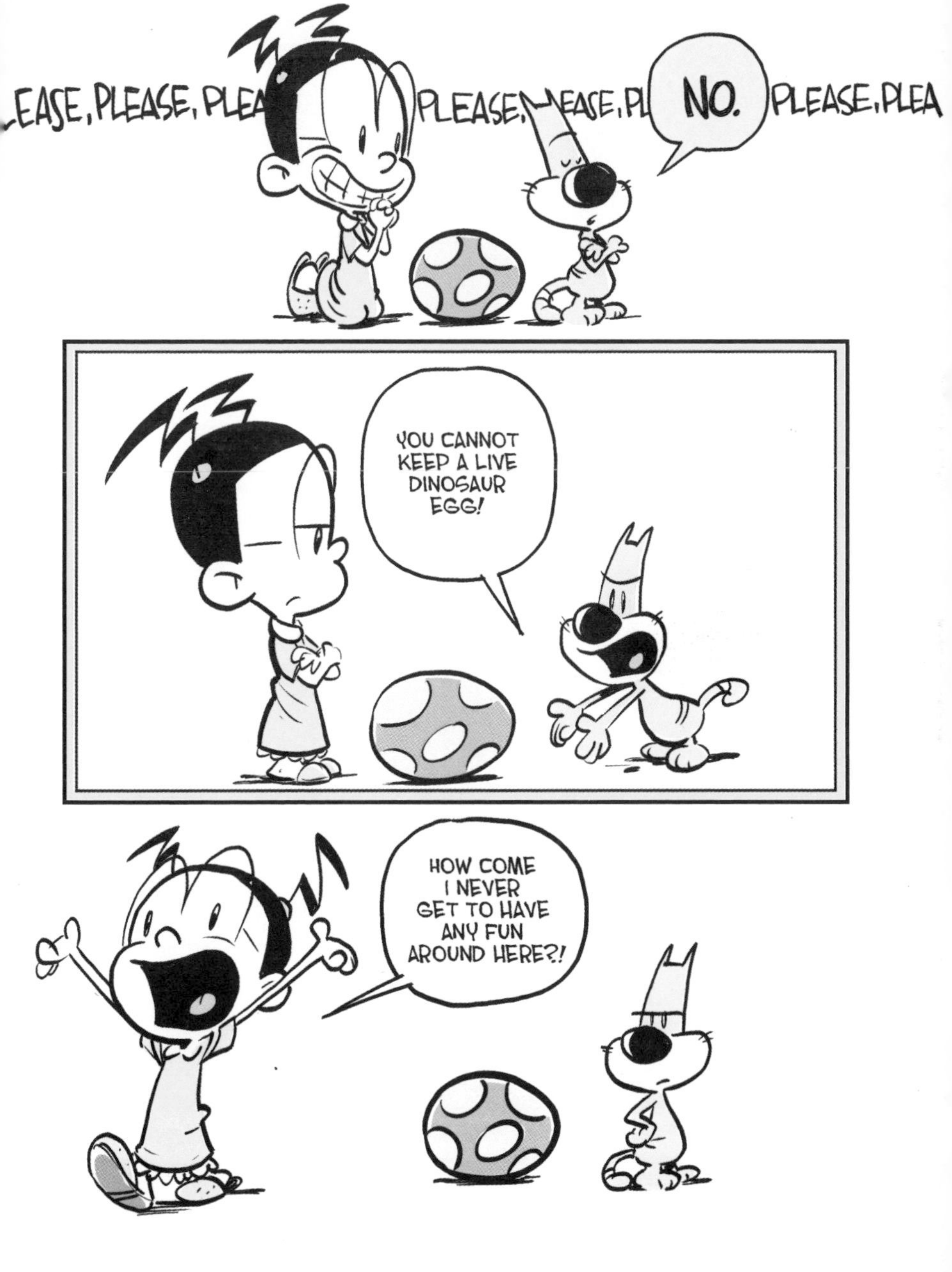
EASE, PLEASE, PLEA
PLEASE, EASE, PL
NO.
PLEASE, PLEA
YOU CANNOT KEEP A LIVE DINOSAUR EGG!
HOW COME I NEVER GET TO HAVE ANY FUN AROUND HERE?!

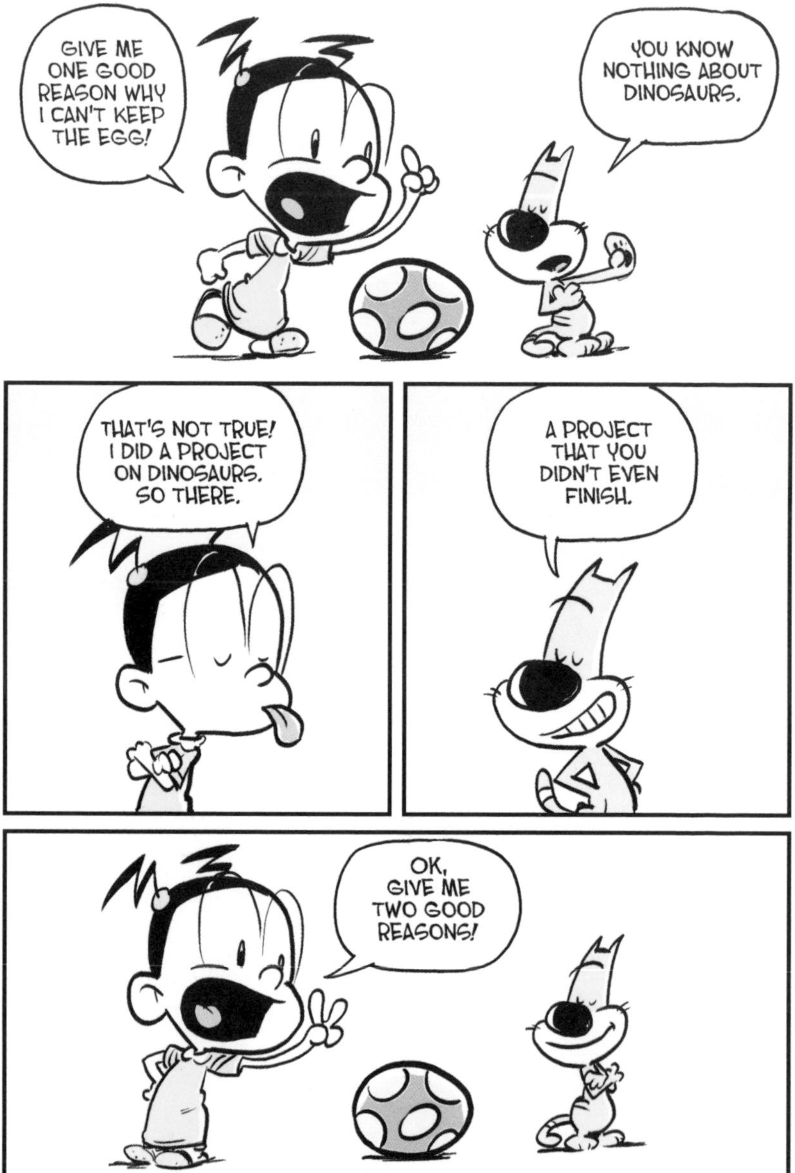
GIVE ME ONE GOOD REASON WHY I CAN'T KEEP THE EGG!
YOU KNOW NOTHING ABOUT DINOSAURS.
THAT'S NOT TRUE! I DID A PROJECT ON DINOSAURS. SO THERE.
A PROJECT THAT YOU DIDN'T EVEN FINISH.
OK, GIVE ME TWO GOOD REASONS!

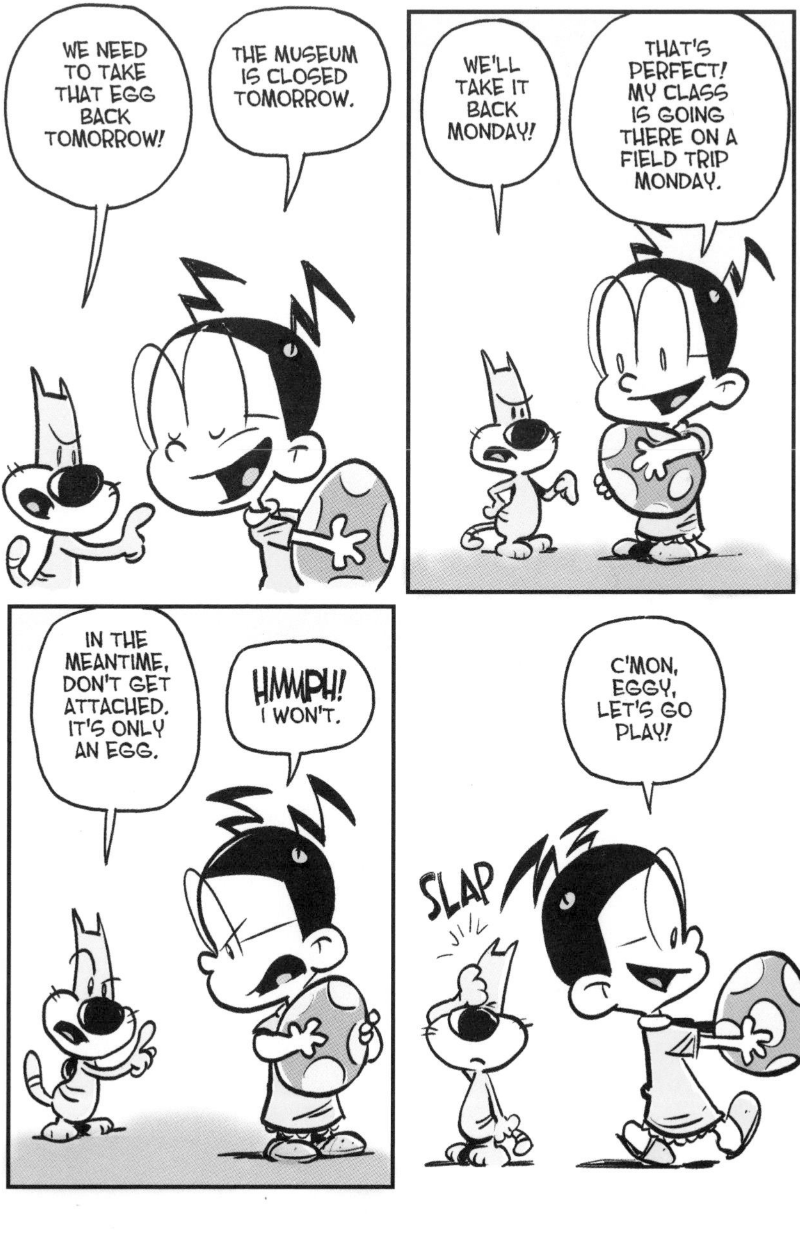
WE NEED TO TAKE THAT EGG BACK TOMORROW!
THE MUSEUM IS CLOSED TOMORROW.
WE'LL TAKE IT BACK MONDAY!
THAT'S PERFECT! MY CLASS IS GOING THERE ON A FIELD TRIP MONDAY.
IN THE MEANTIME, DON'T GET ATTACHED. IT'S ONLY AN EGG.
HMMPH! I WON'T.
C'MON, EGGY, LET'S GO PLAY!
SLAP

The NEXT MORNING

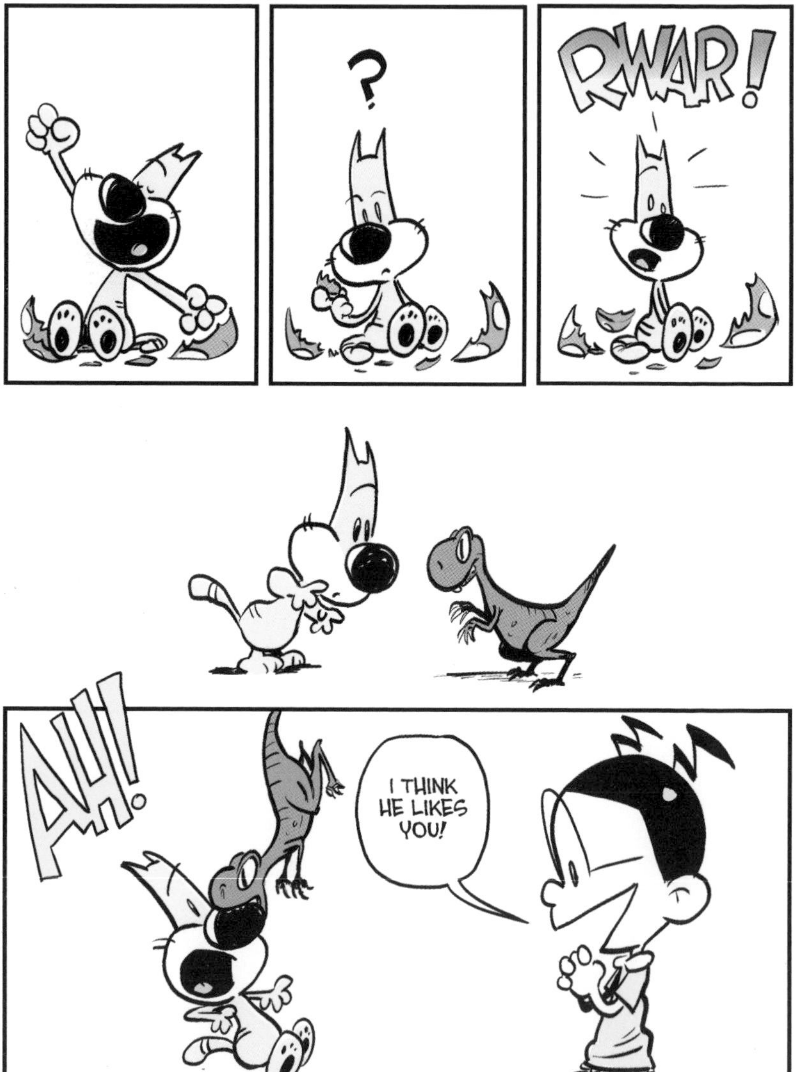
?
RWAR!
AH!
I THINK HE LIKES YOU!

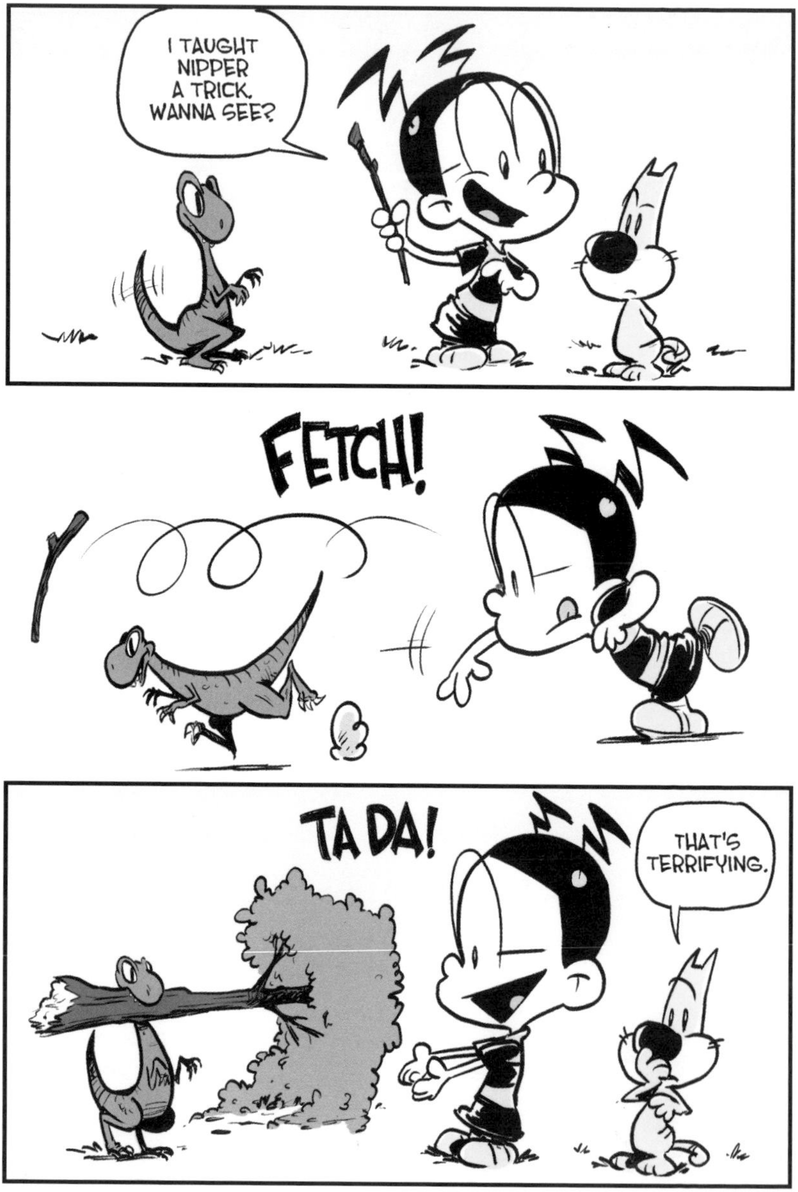
I TAUGHT NIPPER A TRICK. WANNA SEE?
FETCH!
TA DA!
THAT'S TERRIFYING.

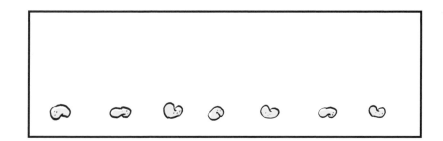

CRUNCH
CRUNCH!

STAY IN
THE BOX
AND I'LL
GET YOU
SOMETHING
TO EAT.

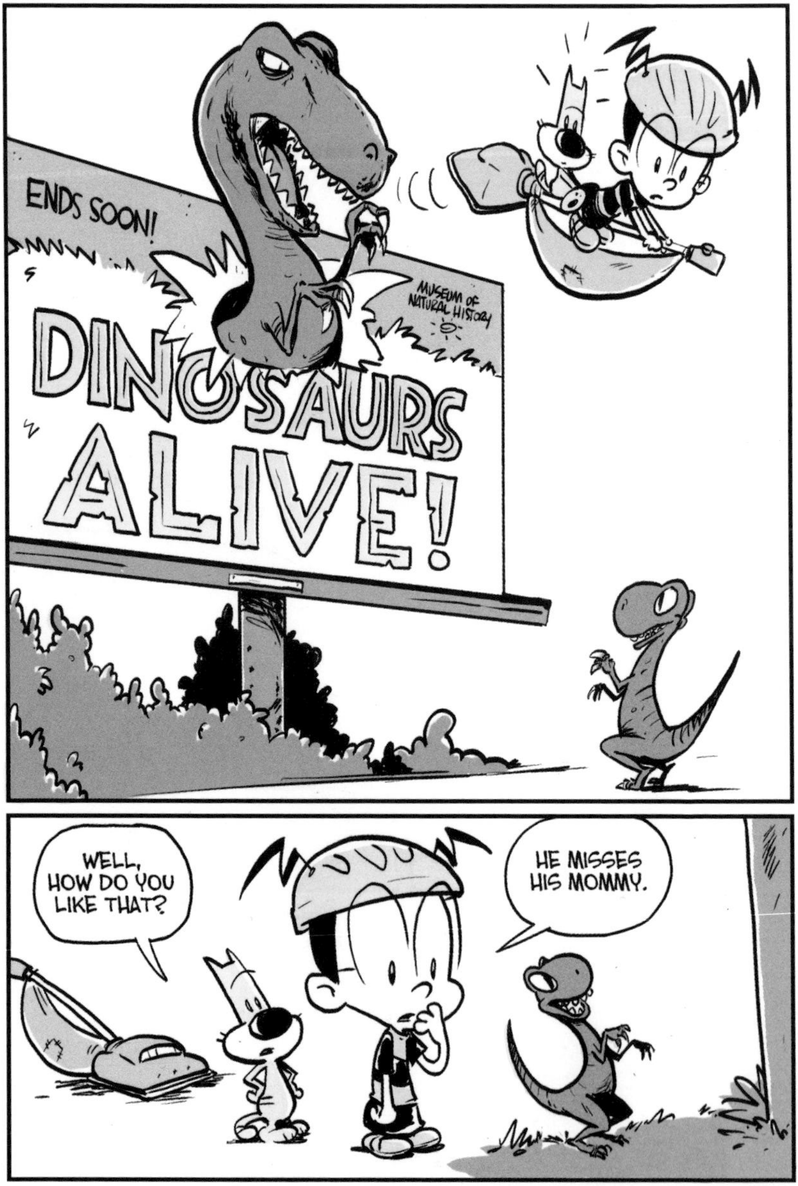
ENDS SOON!
DINOSAURS ALIVE!
MUSEUM OF NATURAL HISTORY
WELL, HOW DO YOU LIKE THAT?
HE MISSES HIS MOMMY.

Getting to Know... Nipper

LIKES

- HUGS
- CHEESE DOODLES
- PLAYING FETCH

DISLIKES

- LOUD NOISES
- METEORS
- BEING AWAY FROM HOME

DID YOU KNOW...

NIPPER IS A THEROPOD.

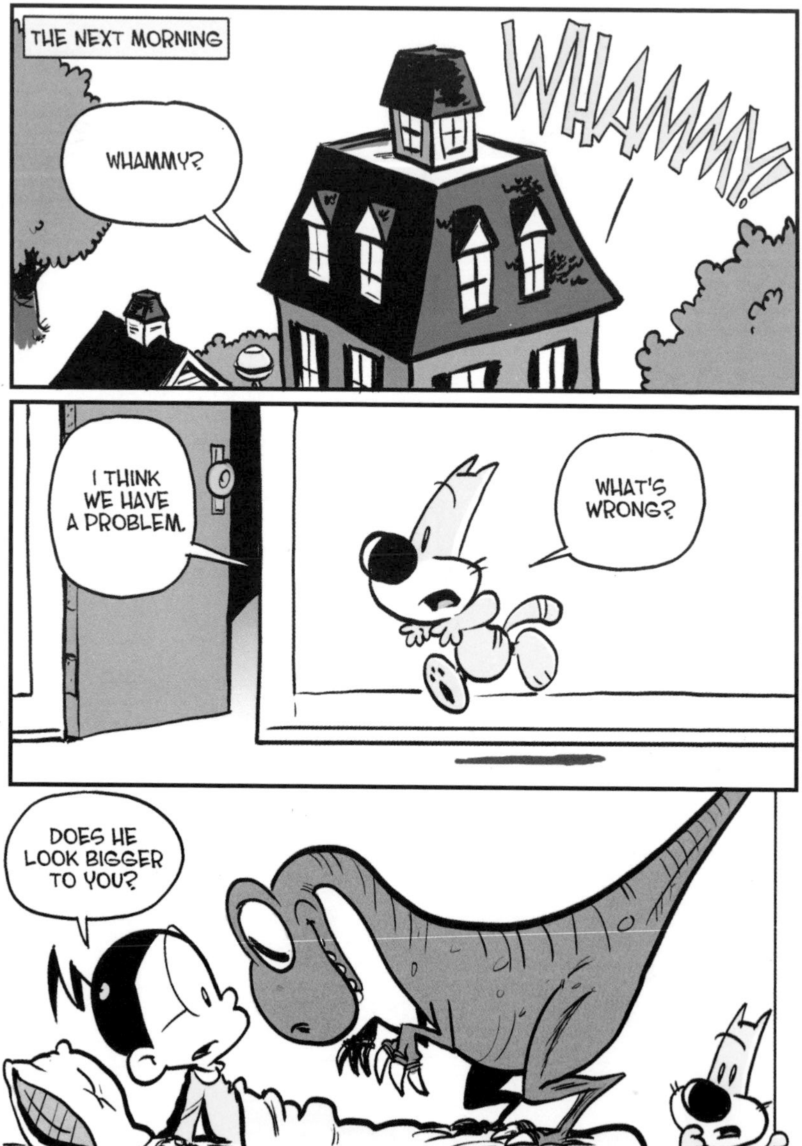
THE NEXT MORNING
WHAMMY?
WHAMMY!
I THINK WE HAVE A PROBLEM.
WHAT'S WRONG?
DOES HE LOOK BIGGER TO YOU?

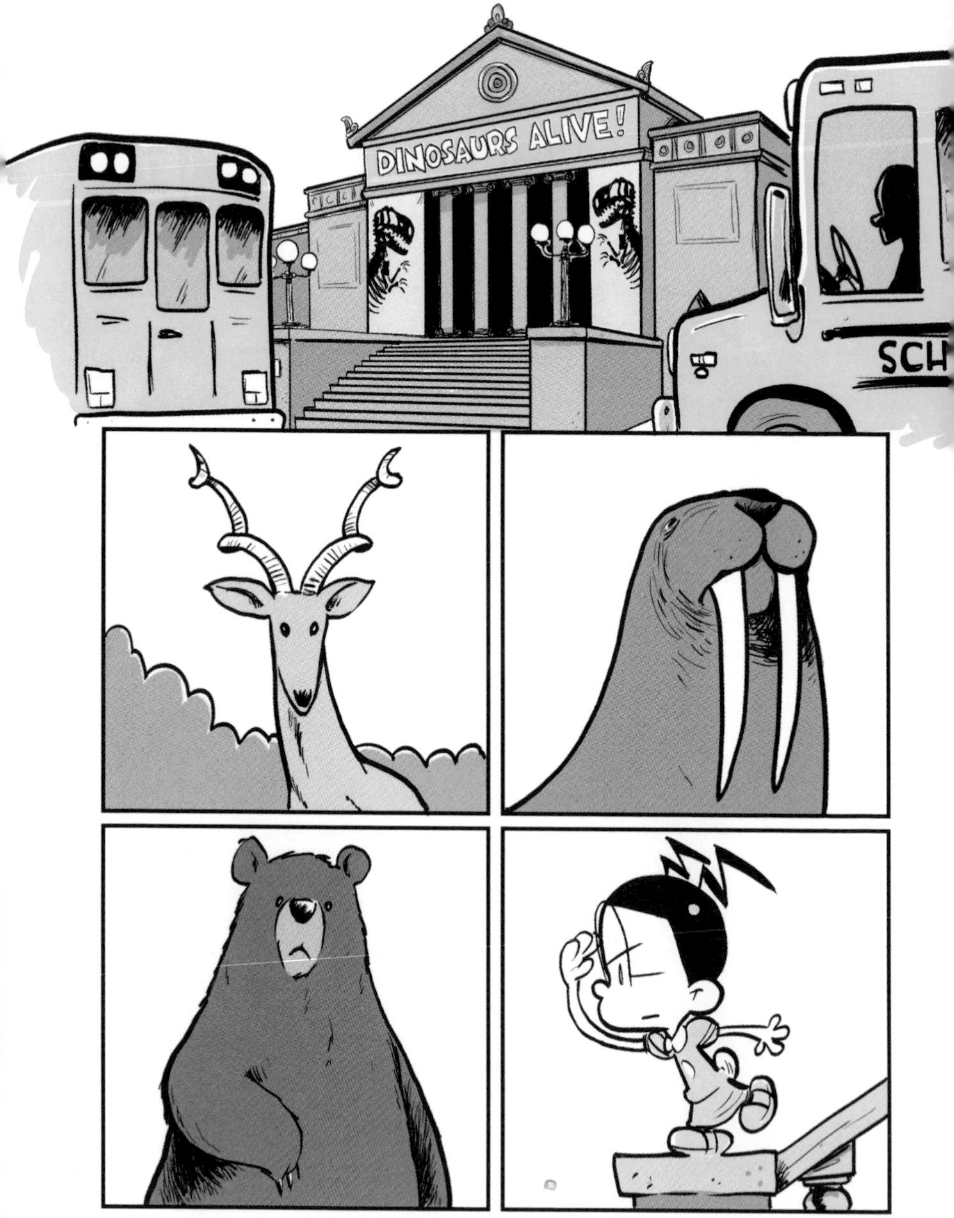
DINOSAURS ALIVE!
SCH

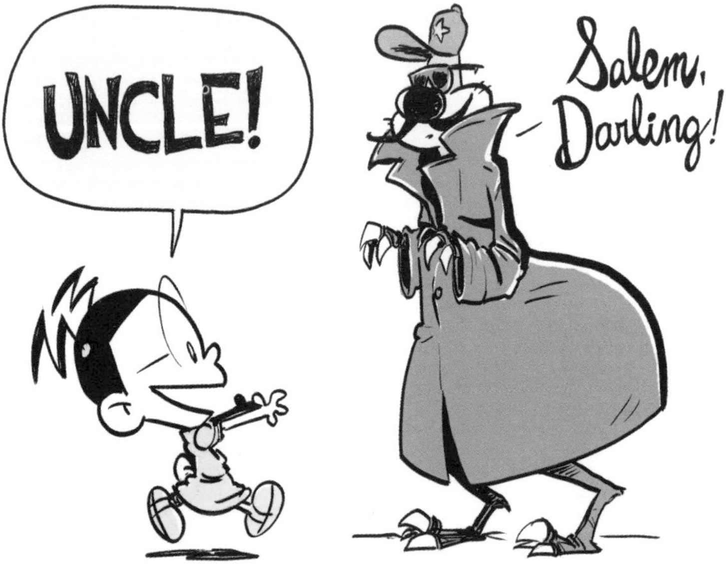
UNCLE!
Salem, Darling!

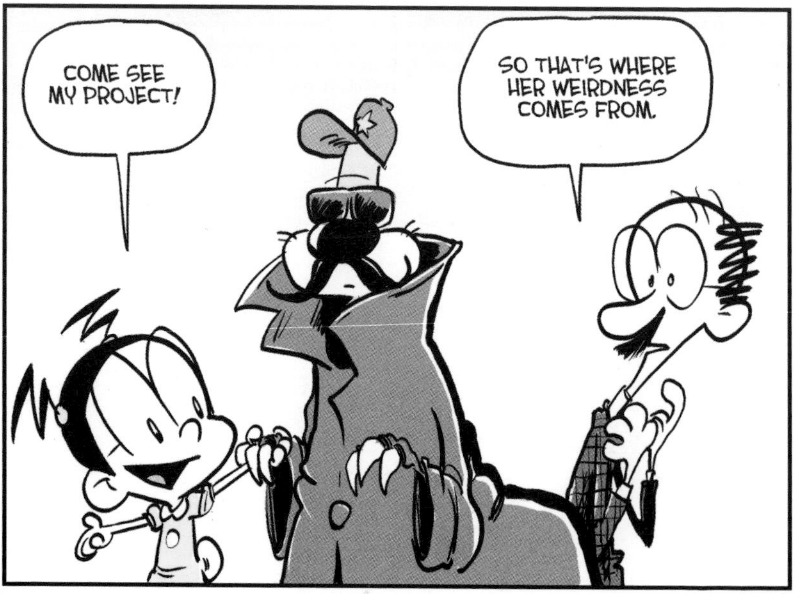
COME SEE MY PROJECT!
SO THAT'S WHERE HER WEIRDNESS COMES FROM.

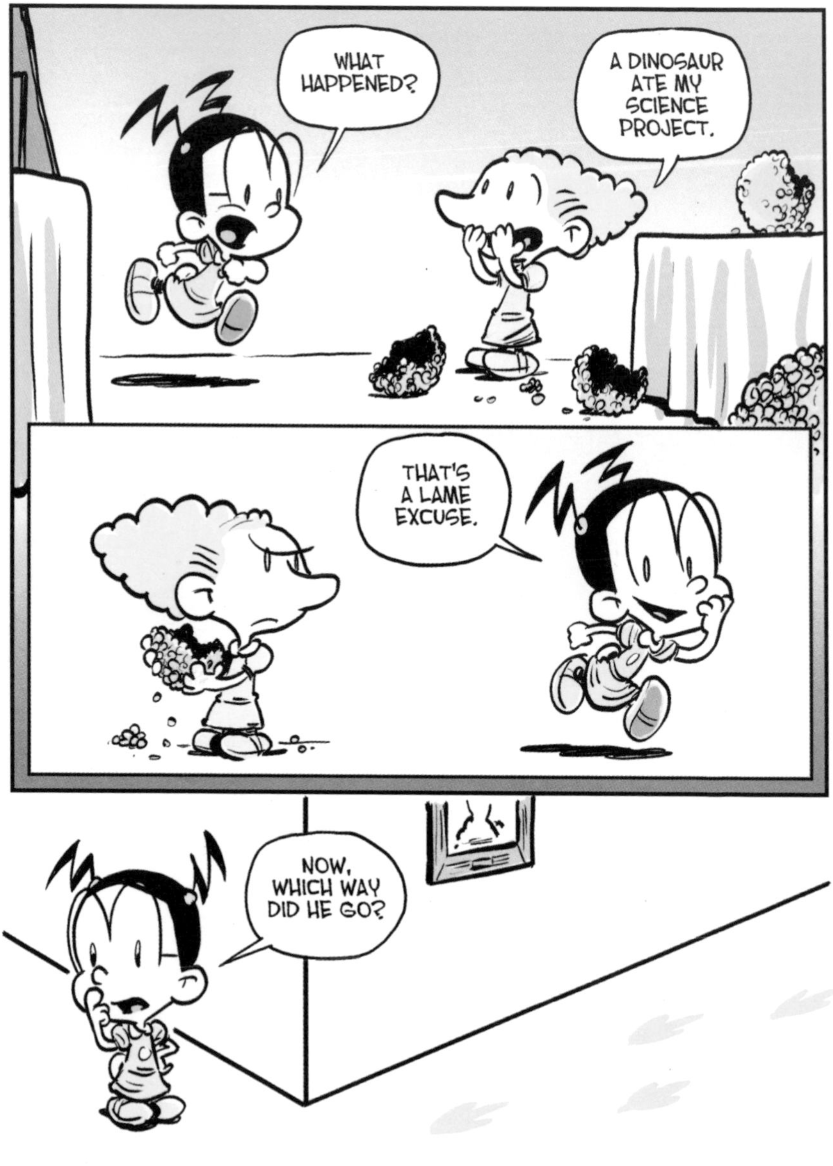
WHAT HAPPENED?
A DINOSAUR ATE MY SCIENCE PROJECT.
THAT'S A LAME EXCUSE.
NOW, WHICH WAY DID HE GO?

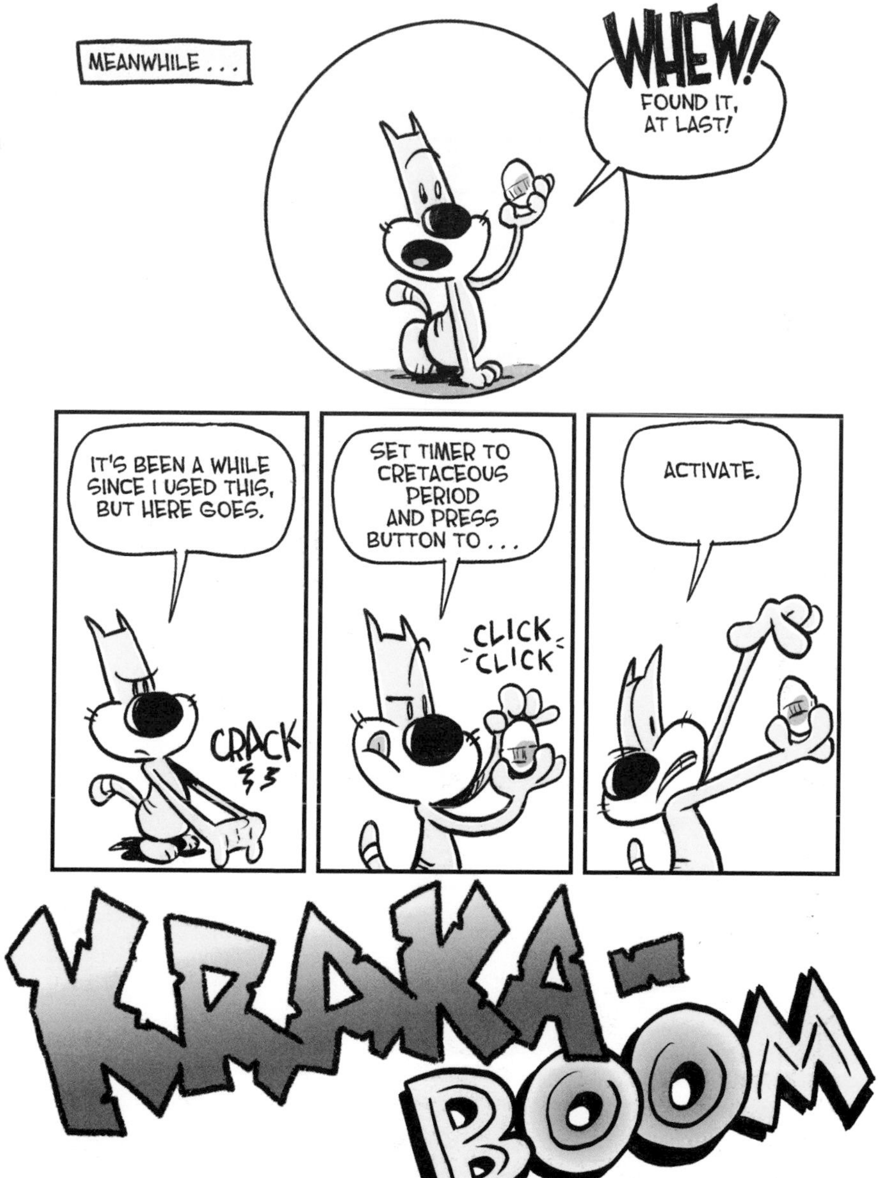
MEANWHILE . . .
WHEW! FOUND IT, AT LAST!
IT'S BEEN A WHILE SINCE I USED THIS, BUT HERE GOES.
CRACK
SET TIMER TO CRETACEOUS PERIOD AND PRESS BUTTON TO . . .
CLICK CLICK
ACTIVATE.
KRAKA-BOOM

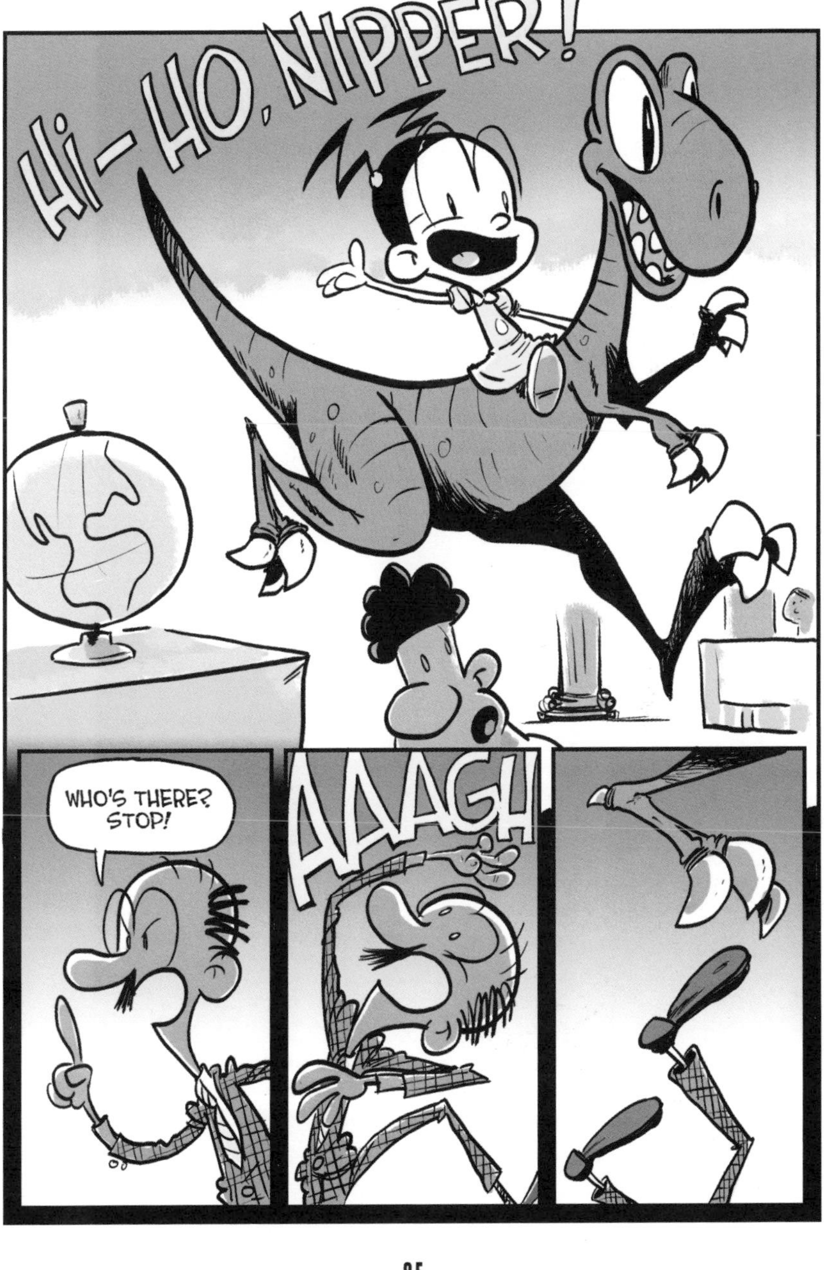
HI-HO, NIPPER!
WHO'S THERE? STOP!
AAAGH!

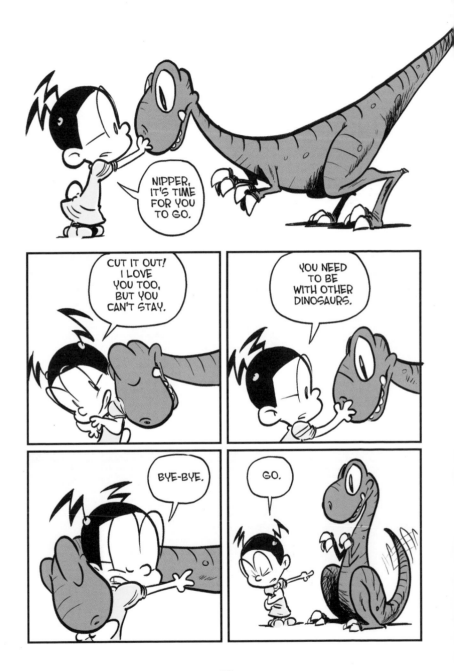

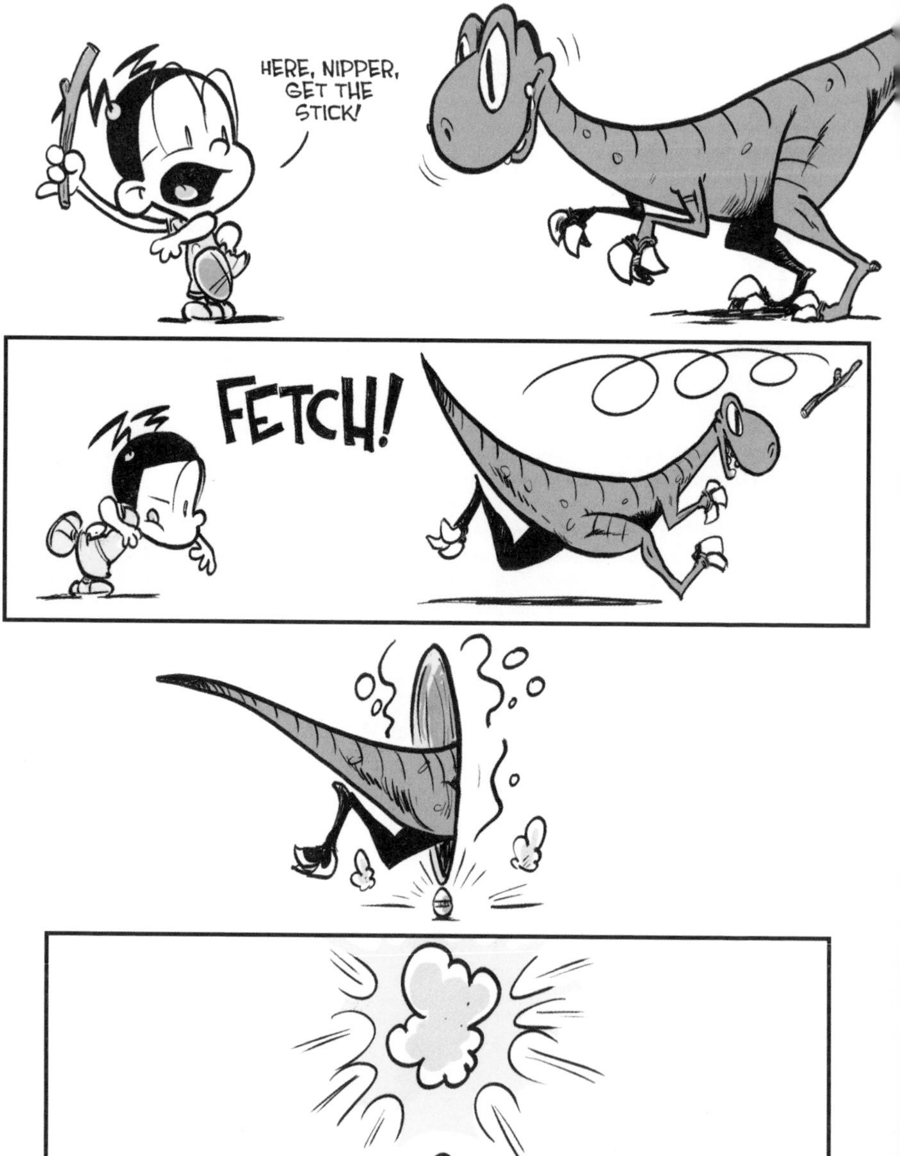
HERE, NIPPER, GET THE STICK!
FETCH!

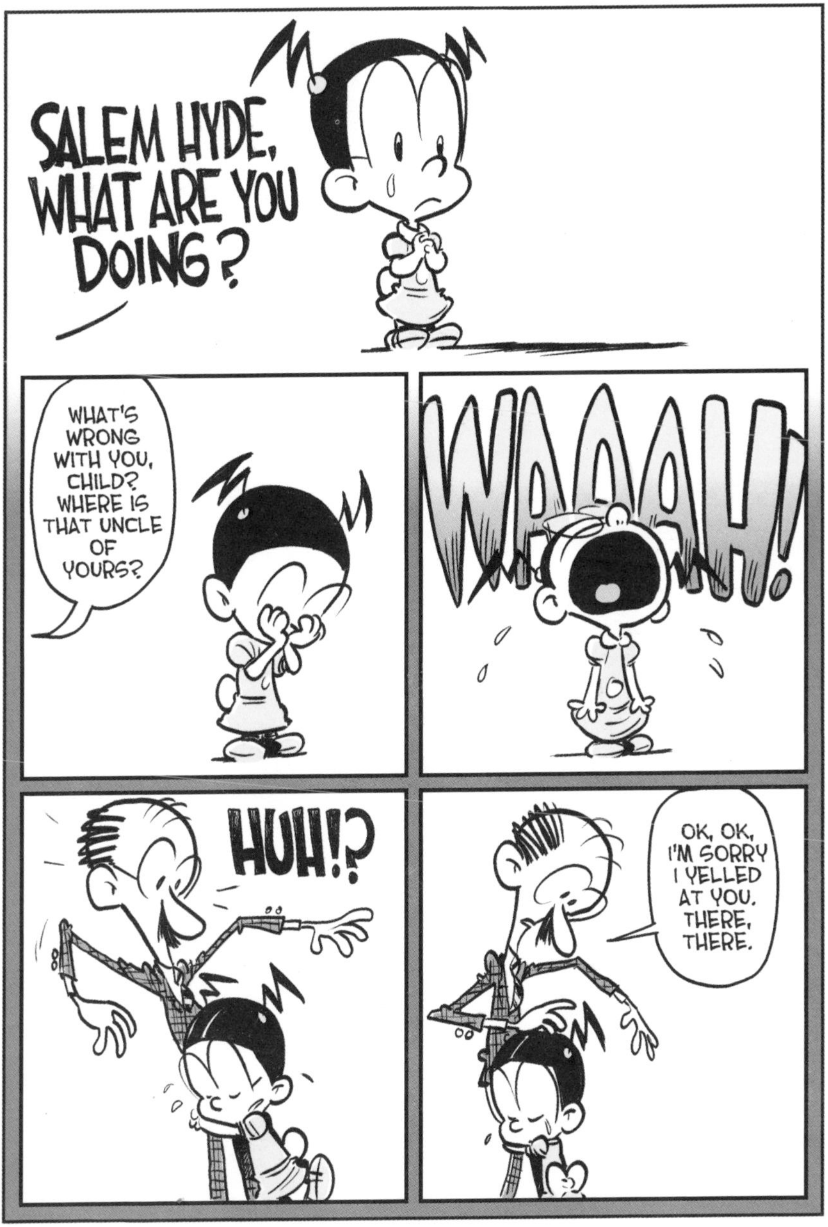
SALEM HYDE, WHAT ARE YOU DOING?
WHAT'S WRONG WITH YOU, CHILD? WHERE IS THAT UNCLE OF YOURS?
WAAAH!
HUH!?
OK, OK, I'M SORRY I YELLED AT YOU. THERE, THERE.

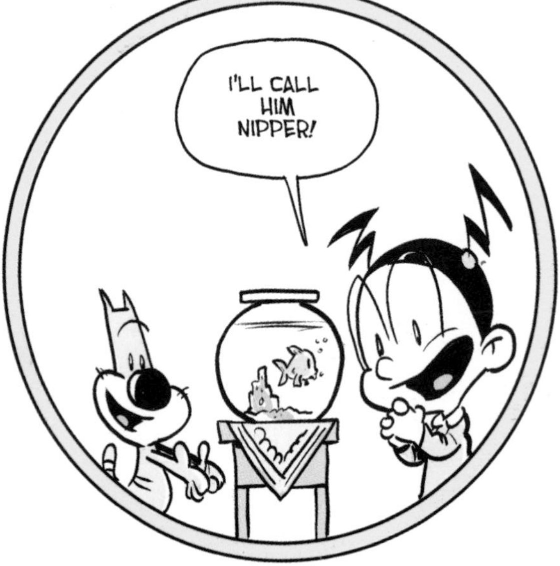
I'LL CALL HIM NIPPER!

Getting to KNOW FRANK CAMMUSO

FRANK LIKES
1. NATURAL HISTORY MUSEUMS
2. CHEESE DOODLES (ALL KINDS)
3. DRAWING DOODLES
4. FIELD TRIPS WITH HIS FAMILY

FRANK DISLIKES
1. SCIENCE PROJECTS
2. MAYONNAISE (ALL KINDS)
3. MOWING THE LAWN
4. CROWDS

FUN FACT: DID YOU KNOW . . . THAT FRANK CAMMUSO'S FAVORITE DINOSAUR IS THE TRICERATOPS?

SPECIAL THANKS TO . . .

Ngoc and Khai, Kathy Leonardo, Nancy Iacovelli, Randy Elliott, Hart Seely, Tom Peyer, Nicole Sclama, Charlie Kochman, Chad Beckerman, Morgan Dubin, and Judy Hansen.

FOR MORE FUN STUFF ABOUT SALEM AND WHAMMY CHECK OUT MY WEBSITE AT . . .

WWW.CAMMUSO.COM

ALSO AVAILABLE

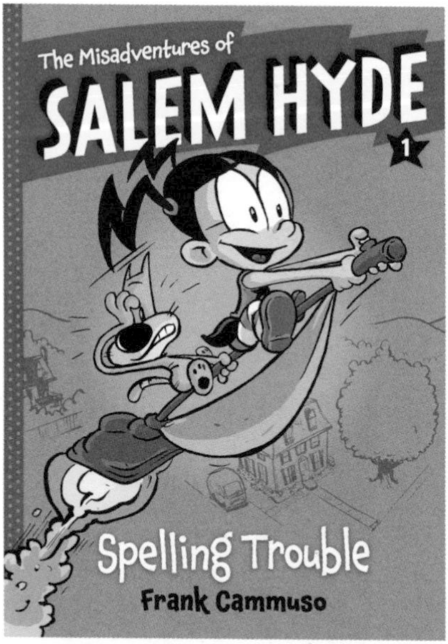
The Misadventures of
SALEM HYDE
1
Spelling Trouble
Frank Cammuso

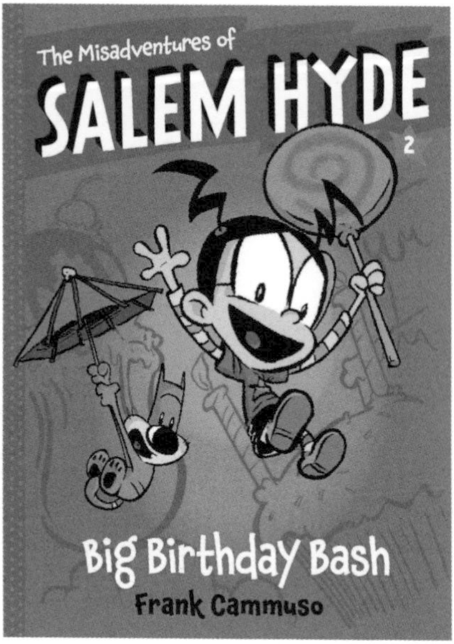
The Misadventures of
SALEM HYDE
2
Big Birthday Bash
Frank Cammuso

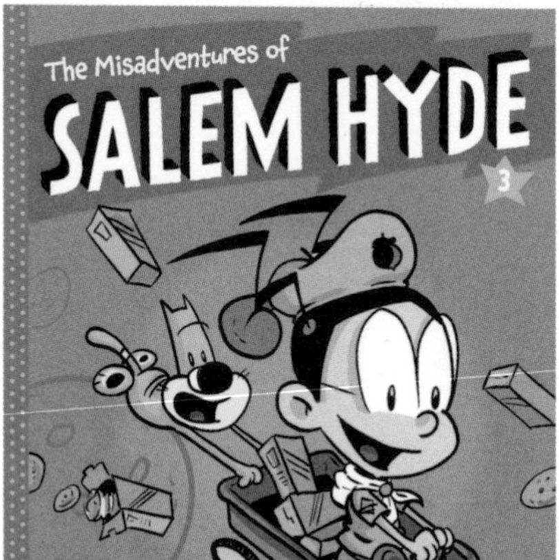
The Misadventures of
SALEM HYDE
3
Cookie Catastrophe
Frank Cammuso

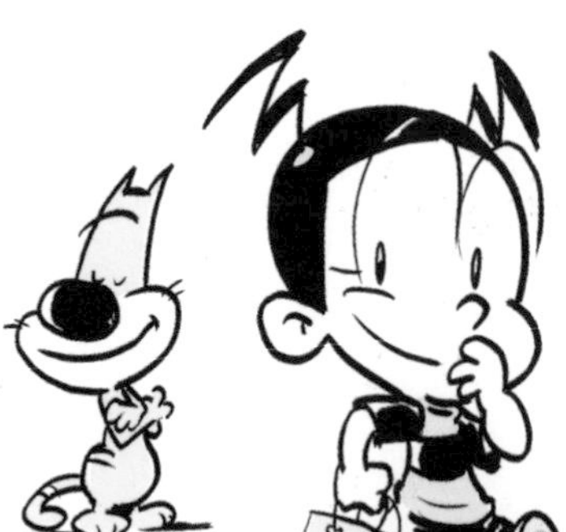

SALEM AND WHAMMY'S
ADVENTURES WILL CONTINUE!